The Hamish Macbeth series

DEATH
OF A
SMUGGLER

A HAMISH MACBETH
-MURDER MYSTERY-

M.C. Beaton

with R.W. Green

GCP

GRAND
CENTRAL

LARGE PRINT

Grand Central Publishing
Hachette Book Group
1290 Avenue of the Americas, New York, NY 10104
grandcentralpublishing.com
twitter.com/grandcentralpub

Published in Great Britain by Constable
First U.S. Edition: February 2025

Grand Central Publishing is a division of Hachette Book Group, Inc. The Grand Central Publishing name and logo is a registered trademark of Hachette Book Group, Inc.

The publisher is not responsible for websites (or their content) that are not owned by the publisher.

The Hachette Speakers Bureau provides a wide range of authors for speaking events. To find out more, go to hachettespeakersbureau.com or email HachetteSpeakers@hbgusa.com.

Grand Central Publishing books may be purchased in bulk for business, educational, or promotional use. For information, please contact your local bookseller or the Hachette Book Group Special Markets Department at special.markets@hbgusa.com.

Library of Congress Cataloging-in-Publication Data has been applied for.

ISBNs: 978-1-5387-4333-1 (hardcover), 978-1-5387-7111-2 (large type), 978-1-5387-4335-5 (ebook)

Printed in the United States of America

LSC-C

Printing 1, 2024

Foreword by R. W. Green

What do you think of when you hear the term VIP? We all know that the three letters stand for Very Important Person, although there are some rather less complimentary definitions, and some that could never be used in polite company! Mostly, however, when we think of a VIP, we think of someone walking the red carpet at a swanky celebrity event, with more flashing lights than a Police Scotland speed camera in disco mode.

Or maybe we think of someone who's given special privileges or special treatment, like the boss of a big company or a major politician. When it comes to VIPs like that, some might tend toward the less polite definitions. Like them or loathe them, however, they still get the VIP care package.

The truth is, there are probably as many different flavors of VIP as there are whiskies in Scotland. Some will be forever in the spotlight, adored by the masses, some are so exclusive that they will only ever be appreciated by the super-rich, some are most definitely an acquired taste, some you take to straight away and some you might never learn to love as long as you live. Unlike coping with celebrities, I can appreciate most kinds of whisky, sometimes appreciating them well into the wee small hours.

In the remote, fictional, Highland village of Lochdubh, situated on a sea loch off the Minch, a very real Atlantic channel that separates mainland Scotland from the islands of the Outer Hebrides, I think that Hamish Macbeth is a special sort of VIP. He certainly doesn't seek out the limelight and he definitely prefers living a quiet life to having people fussing around him. He doesn't like to draw attention to himself, especially when it comes to senior police officers, always wary of the danger of promotion. Were he to rise above his rank of sergeant, he'd be forced to move out of his little police station in

Lochdubh. That would be a disaster. That would ruin his whole life. Consequently, he seldom even claims credit for the work that he does, declining recognition, preferring to pass the glory up the chain of command where others can wallow in it.

So how does that make Hamish a VIP? Well, I think he's the most fundamental, most indispensable of all VIPs. Hamish is a Very Important Person within his local community, even though many of the locals will never appreciate him nearly as much as he, and I, appreciate a wee dram. There we go again—another reference to whisky. Seems writing about it is like drinking it—it's hard to know when to stop! Nevertheless, Hamish cares about Lochdubh and the people who live there and he does whatever it takes to keep everything in the area ticking over just the way it should. That does not, however, mean he's some kind of saint.

When I first began working with M. C. Beaton (Marion) a few years ago, she was very keen to point out that Hamish was an honest, ethical policeman who obeyed the law but was not above a little dishonest, unethical lawbreaking under the right circumstances. Poaching the odd salmon, grouse, pheasant or even a deer were things, according to Marion, that Hamish might be tempted to do from time to time. How tempting, then, would it be for him to help himself to some smuggled whisky? Were it to be handed over as evidence, after all, it would eventually be poured away. Rather than have it go to waste, of course VIP Macbeth would "liberate" it! As it's not a hugely appalling act of villainy, I'm sure Marion would approve of Hamish's behavior, especially as he doesn't keep all of his ill-gotten gains to himself. There are others he encounters who also enjoy a dram or two!

Since we're now talking about whisky again, and smuggled whisky in particular, we might as well look at its long history as a smuggled, or even illicitly produced, item. Whisky has been made in Scotland for over six centuries. The Irish claim to have been making it for longer and there's plenty of evidence to back their claim, so we owe them a big vote of thanks for that—the more the merrier! Scotch whisky, of course, can only be produced in Scotland. It was first made by farmers who grew barley, which fared well in the Scottish climate, to feed their families and their cattle. Any surplus was turned into whisky.

Eventually, distilling whisky became more lucrative than raising cattle and governments of the day quickly realized the revenue that could be generated by levying a tax on whisky production. The distillers took to the hills, quite literally, and it's been estimated that, by the 1820s, there may have been as many as fourteen thousand secret stills in operation up in the mountains, producing whisky that the government couldn't keep tabs on. While as much as half the whisky drunk in Scotland was consumed without benefit to the taxman, just as much was being smuggled south across the border into England, the distillers playing a constant and dangerous game evading the revenue men.

In 1823, the Excise Act made it more profitable for distillers to produce their whisky legally and smuggling began to die out. Did it die out completely? Not a chance! Is today's taxman getting his full cut? Again, not a chance! Scotch whisky distillers are now producing more whisky than ever before, most of it for export. More than fifty bottles of Scotch are shipped out of Scotland *every second* in an export trade worth £6 billion.

The distillers, of course, keep everything absolutely correct and above board, but once the whisky passes into the market, it can end up in the hands of unscrupulous traders. Whisky designated for export is exempt from VAT and other UK duty, meaning that if it can be smuggled back into the country, criminals can make substantial profits. There's also something called "diversion fraud," where whisky designated for export never actually leaves the UK. Such illegal Scotch, of course, represents just a tiny percentage of the market.

Smuggling Scotch back into Scotland, therefore, isn't as weird as it might first seem. Hamish's brush with a mysterious, small-time smuggler leaves him with a perplexing murder to solve under the vigilant eyes of an equally mysterious senior police officer. It also pitches him in with the despicable DCI Blair, who is his sworn enemy. Their interaction doesn't always go entirely as you might expect this time round.

Things, however, aren't all bad for Hamish. This adventure sees him managing to maintain his relationship with paramedic Claire and we also have the return of an old friend as his new constable. That happy return is, unfortunately, marred by a secret lurking in the background. Eventually, Hamish demands to know the truth and can scarcely believe his ears when he hears it!

The murder, of course, is his top priority and he knows he has to clear up the crime quickly to get all the interlopers off his patch and to protect his local community.

Hamish is, after all, a Very Important Policeman in Lochdubh.

I'll drink to that!

Rod Green, 2025

Chapter One

If you wake at midnight, and hear a
* horse's feet,*
Don't go drawing back the blind, or look-
* ing in the street;*
Them that ask no questions isn't told a lie.
Watch the wall, my darling, while the
* Gentlemen go by!*
          Rudyard Kipling, "A Smuggler's
                              Song" (1906)

At first it seemed there was silence. When the small boat's outboard motor stopped, for a brief moment there was nothing else to be heard. Then, as if creeping into the night air to take the place of the motor's buzz, the lapping of the water against the prow of the wooden dinghy made itself apparent to the young woman perched on the bench seat. Then came the splash of the ripples against the nearby rocks and the gentle rush of waves breaking on the beach ahead.

Looking back out across the loch, she could see the dark shape of a larger boat, a fishing boat, lying at anchor in deeper water. The fishing boat's lights were extinguished, but it was still clearly visible in the moonlight, casting a shadow that dulled the ribbons of silver drifting on the loch's surface. On a second bench, facing forward, sat a dark-haired man huddled in a bulky black jacket against the chill night air. Just behind him, an older, gray-bearded man was hunched at the tiller, guiding the dinghy to shore. Between them was stacked a cargo of cardboard boxes.

Unlike the men, the woman sat tall, her back straight. In the moonlight, her pale features and forlorn expression made her look almost ghostlike, her sadness sharpened by the tear threatening to tumble from the corner of her eye. She gave her head a shake to banish the tear. The men would surely never notice if she were to break down and cry but she was determined that they should never have even the slightest chance of seeing her do so. She gripped a small rucksack she was holding in her lap, clenching her fists around its straps, gazing out into the blackness beyond the fishing boat. Somewhere out there, across almost 3,500 miles of ocean, lay America. New York—that's where they said she would start a new life. A visa, an apartment, new clothes and a modeling contract were what she had been promised. That was what she had paid for, not a furtive landing on a dismal beach in the middle of night in the middle of nowhere. Where were they anyway? Scotland? What did that mean to her? What did she know of Scotland? Nothing—except that it was not New York!

The bow of the dinghy crunched on the beach, grinding to a halt, and the young woman swayed a little as the boat lurched.

"You, Kira, or whatever your name is," grunted the man in the black jacket, glowering at the young woman and jerking his thumb toward the water, "ower the side, now!"

Kira could see only the bow of the dinghy had grounded. The rest was still floating free in water that looked at least knee-deep.

3

M. C. BEATON

"What? In water?" Kira said, frowning at him.

"Aye, it'll no' kill you," the man snapped. "Get a move on!"

Flinging her rucksack over the bow and clear of the water onto the beach, she lowered herself over the side. The water was bitterly cold, and the jeans she was wearing offered no protection, soaking through immediately. She'd been wrong about it being knee-deep. It came up almost to her waist.

"Take this," the man ordered, standing in the boat to pass her a large cardboard box, the clink of glass betraying its contents as bottles.

Kira reached up to accept the heavy box from the man and then, just as he turned to take another box from the bearded man, she staggered sideways as if by accident, slamming her shoulder into the side of the dinghy, causing it to rock violently.

"Be careful, you clumsy…ohhhhh!" the man let out a groan of dread, then pitched backward into the water, still clutching the box. A little further out than the woman, in slightly deeper water, for a moment he submerged completely

4

then broke the surface again, howling with fury and struggling to find his balance, the box gone. Kira cast her box aside, took two steps toward him and grabbed him under the arms, manhandling him toward the shore.

"Never mind me!" he roared, glancing from her sinking box to where his had disappeared. "Save the whisky!"

She abruptly let him go and he sank even faster than the cases of whisky. Once he'd found his feet again, he steadied himself with a hand on the side of the boat. The bearded man looked down at him with concern.

"Are you all right there?" he asked slowly.

"Och, aye!" the man in the water spluttered, his teeth chattering. "I'm fair enjoying a wee midnight dip!"

"Ahh..." said the man in the boat, nodding wisely. "That would be yon sarcasm I'm ay hearing about."

"We need to get those boxes afore they start falling apart! You can..." He turned toward Kira, but she was nowhere to be seen. "Where the hell has she gone?"

"No sign o' her on the beach," reported the bearded man, craning his neck. "Looks like she's scarpered."

"Stupid bitch! She'll no' get far without…" He patted his breast pocket and cursed. "Damn her! She's lifted my wallet and the passports from inside my coat!"

"I guess we'll no' be seeing her again, then."

The man in the water rested his head on the side of the dinghy and ran a hand through his hair, the wet gold of the rings on his fingers glinting in the moonlight. Water drained off his head to run down his face. He sighed, then looked out toward the fishing boat.

"We'll be seeing her again, all right," he grumbled, stripping off his jacket. "We still have the other girl out there on the boat. She'll no' abandon her wee friend. Now, let's get that whisky ashore afore I freeze to death."

In a small copse of trees close to the shore, Kira crouched behind a thicket of alder, shivering as she watched the men bringing the cases of whisky ashore, stacking them on the beach. When the dinghy headed back out to the fishing boat, she took the opportunity to kick off her white sports shoes, then stripped off her jeans, underwear and socks. She rubbed her legs vigorously to dry them and to try to warm herself before taking dry clothes from her rucksack. Dressing quickly, she stuffed the wet clothes into the bag, then crammed her feet back into the sodden shoes. She knew they would take some time to dry out and, in the meantime, her feet would be damp, but she had to be ready to move—ready to make a run for it if necessary. Suffering the discomfort of cold, wet feet was better than falling back into the hands of those men.

She could hear them reach the fishing boat, the dinghy's motor cutting out again, although she wasn't able to see the bigger boat from her hiding place. She thought about moving to find a better vantage spot, then dismissed the idea. She wasn't familiar with the territory and she didn't want to risk being spotted. She would wait. The boxes were on the beach and she knew the men would soon be back with more. Just a few minutes later, she heard the drone of the outboard motor pushing the dinghy back toward the beach. In the still of the night, it sounded disturbingly loud, the sound clamoring across the water. Surely someone would hear them? On this quiet stretch of coast, however, it seemed there were very few who might hear. She could see what appeared to be a large house some way off on the higher ground beyond the beach and a couple of small cottages even farther away. In the weak moonlight it was difficult to tell how far they were, but there were certainly no lights shining from distant windows. The countryside was dormant.

When the dinghy reappeared, making its way back toward the beach, she could see the dark shapes of the two men and, sitting in the bow just where she had been, a slimmer figure—Elena. The two women had endured a long, arduous journey from Latvia together to reach this shore. She watched in silence, then cursed the men for forcing Elena into the water to help unload even more cases of whisky. When they were finished, the bearded man walked off up the beach and she heard the sound of a car being started. A four-wheel-drive pickup truck then appeared from where a track cut down onto the beach, crossing the sand and pebbles to the stacked whisky cases, which were duly loaded onto the truck. Elena was then bundled into the passenger seat. From her hiding place in the trees, Kira saw her friend look round in panic. Even from a distance the desperation on Elena's face was obvious. She wanted to call out, to wave, to tell Elena not to be frightened, to tell her that she would come for her and everything would be fine, but all she could do was to watch and wait.

The man in the black jacket climbed back into the dinghy, the bearded man pushed it off the beach and the motor started, taking it out again toward the fishing boat. The bearded man then got behind the wheel of the truck, driving it up onto the track in the direction of the large house where it disappeared from sight, although a light soon appeared in one of the building's windows. Kira stared at the window. Was Elena being held there? Was that house the reason why they had come ashore on this particular stretch of beach? She had to get to the house to find out.

At that moment, she heard the fishing boat's

engine start up. Tentatively, she crept out of the woods and, on seeing the boat heading toward the mouth of the loch, trailing the dinghy behind it, she broke cover and made for the track. Keeping low and moving swiftly, she stayed close to the drystone wall edging the track, trying to sink into its darkest shadows. While she moved, all she could hear was the sound of her own breathing and an alien squelching noise from her shoes. When she paused to listen, there was nothing to hear but the waves sweeping the beach and the distant rumble of the fishing-boat engine.

It took just a few minutes to reach the open gate leading to the large building. She could now see that it was some sort of pub with a sign above the door that read: LOCH MUIR INN. Treading lightly, she inched toward the building, flattening herself against the wall beside the window showing a light. She risked a glance inside and saw Elena standing at a kitchen worktop side-by-side with the bearded man, who was preparing a meal. Her friend had changed out of her wet clothes, now looking dry and warm.

Kira slunk back to the gate, sinking down

into the shadows. Elena had looked like she was about to be fed and the inn seemed warm and comfortable. They had been shipped across Europe together in trucks and vans, then transferred from one boat to another. Elena was as exhausted as she was herself. She would leave her there, at least for tonight. Right now, she had to find somewhere she could shelter. She looked up at the moon, watching a cluster of light clouds drifting across its face. It was starting to feel like it might rain.

Only a few miles farther north in Lochdubh, Hamish Macbeth stood in his small back garden, looking up at the clouds mustering their strength, determined to obscure the moon.

"Looks like we could have a spot o' rain afore morning, Sonsie," he said, smiling at his wildcat, which gazed back at him with wide, yellow eyes. Sonsie was relaxing on the roof of his shed, enjoying the nervous clucking of the chickens tucked away safely inside for the night. It always amazed him that Sonsie never went for his birds.

She was a wildcat, after all, although everyone in the village preferred to think of her simply as an overgrown tabby. Keeping a wildcat, an endangered species, was strictly against the law, so the local policeman surely wouldn't have one, would he? Whatever anyone else thought, Hamish was devoted to Sonsie. He reached out to stroke her sleek fur. He was one of only a select few she permitted to touch her. "You wouldn't want one o' those daft chickens, would you, lass? You like your food to come from the kitchen, and there's no point going for a chicken when you've a full belly, eh? Come on, then. Time for bed."

Hamish strolled into his kitchen and the big cat leapt down from the shed, following at his heels, waiting patiently while he closed the back door, then falling in behind him again as he climbed the stairs.

"I thought you were never coming up," came a voice from the dimly lit bedroom when he opened the door. "Come to bed, Hamish. I've to be out early in the morning."

Claire was a paramedic Hamish had met through work. The two had grown close over the

12

past few months and their romance had become the talk of the village.

"Aye, I was just taking a last wee look out across the loch," Hamish said, undressing and lifting a reluctant, sleepy Lugs off the bed. The dog opened his eyes just long enough to give Hamish a weary look, a soft ear-lick and a heavy sigh. Hamish laid Lugs on the floor where he curled up beside Sonsie.

"We'll maybe no' have so many nights like this when we've no' got the place to ourselves," Claire said, snuggling into his side once Hamish had switched off the bedside light and settled beneath the duvet. "It won't be the same once your new constable gets here."

"I don't see why not," Hamish replied, chuckling. "He'll be in the other bedroom, no' in here wi' us!"

"Aye, but it might be a wee bit embarrassing," Claire said, laughing softly. "We've no idea who he is or what he'll be like. It will be a 'he,' won't it?"

"Seems it's a bloke," Hamish admitted. "The message I got earlier this evening only said the one who was coming here had been reassigned, no' who was coming in his place, but it did say 'he' would be here in the morning."

"Then we'd best make the most o' our last night alone," Claire said, reaching across to kiss him.

When the sun rose the following morning, the waters of Loch Dubh reflected a sky full of clouds that bore the dark gray and blue bruises of an Atlantic storm. Trundling toward the yellow light in the east, the clouds dragged across the summits of the mountains surrounding the loch, tearing themselves apart on the rocky summits and spilling the last of their rain in the forested slopes.

By the time Claire trotted downstairs just after seven, Hamish was already in the kitchen. Having fed Lugs and Sonsie, he was preparing a breakfast of sausage, bacon and eggs that Claire reluctantly had to refuse as she started her shift at Braikie Hospital at eight. She gave him a kiss, a smile and a promise to make it up to him later. When she hurried outside to her car, she saw a tall, well-built, young police officer in uniform walking in from the street, carrying a couple of large holdalls. At first, she thought only that Hamish's new constable was reporting bright and early. Then, she frowned a little, wondering why she felt she knew him. Then, when she saw him smile, she knew exactly who he was and immediately wished she could stay for breakfast, if only to see the look on Hamish's face.

"I've got to rush," she said, treating him to a huge, welcoming smile and reaching up to give him a hug, at which point he dropped his bags, "but you're in luck—he's got breakfast on the go."

The young man grinned, made her promise to meet later for a drink and a catch-up, then straightened his black Police Scotland top, picked up his bags and headed for the kitchen door.

"Sergeant Macbeth," he said, standing in the doorway to introduce himself. "Constable David Forbes. I believe you're expecting me."

In a whirlwind of delight, Lugs suddenly transformed himself from a politely seated, food-begging statue of a dog into a bounding, tail-wagging lick monster, joyously planting his big paws on the newcomer's chest in a desperate effort to reach high enough to slobber all over his face and ears. Laughing, the young man set his bags down to try to defend himself. Sonsie, curled comfortably in her basket, looked up from her third snooze of the morning, blinked twice to check she recognized the young man then gave a sedate nod of welcome. She was pretty sure she remembered him as a friend, but it simply wouldn't do for her to go bananas like the idiot dog.

"Davey!" Hamish dropped the wooden spatula he was using to turn the sausages in the pan and wiped his hands on a tea towel. "I was *not* expecting you, but I am right glad to see you, laddie!"

He crossed the kitchen in a single stride, reached out to shake Davey's hand then hesitated, laughed and engulfed the young man in a bear hug.

"Steady on, Hamish!" Davey laughed. "You're making poor Lugs properly jealous!"

"I see you're still into pumping iron and making muscles," Hamish said, slapping Davey's bulging biceps.

"Aye, and I got back into the rugby again

down south for a while," Davey replied. "It wasn't all hard work and no play."

"Come away in and sit yourself down, Davey," Hamish said, returning to his spitting frying pan. "I've some breakfast just about ready and there's coffee made fresh."

"I saw Claire on my way in," Davey said, sitting at the kitchen table and ruffling Lugs's ears. "So you two are..."

"She's very special to me," Hamish said with a hint of a warning that Davey should be careful what he said next.

"I'm glad," Davey said, grinning. "The whole village was talking about what a fine couple you made just before I left."

"Aye, well, a lot's happened since you left," Hamish said, serving up two steaming plates of sausage, bacon and eggs. "You were in plain-clothes back then. You were a detective constable set on a career wi' the CID in Edinburgh. What on Earth brings you back up here, in uniform?"

"Maybe I wasn't ready for the Edinburgh job," Davey said, his grin collapsing into a half-hearted smile. "Being a detective isn't all it's cracked up to be. There's an awful lot of sitting about, watching CCTV footage and the like. I felt like I needed a proper spell of frontline policing before I started down the detective path."

Hamish knew he was lying. He had been lied to by some of the most devious scunners ever to draw breath and he had a finely tuned sense of what was true and what was not. Like all good lies, there was a grain of truth in what Davey had just said, but it couldn't disguise the fabrication. Davey's smile was begging Hamish not to press him further and, in less than a heartbeat, Hamish decided to move on. Davey would give him the truth sooner or later.

"Well, I'm no' sure anyone would call Lochdubh 'frontline,'" Hamish said, laughing, "but there will be plenty of work for us once the winter starts to take hold, so I'm right pleased to see you."

"And I'm very happy to be back," Davey said, tucking into his breakfast.

Kira woke when the thin light of dawn filtered through the grime on the window of the shed in which she had taken shelter the night before. She yawned, rubbing her eyes, and flung off the musty blanket she had found. She couldn't wait to get out in the fresh air to banish its smell from her clothes. Her shoes, sitting on the floor near the door, seemed almost to have dried out, so she slipped them on. Walking would rid them of their lingering dampness. Then she heard a noise outside and opened the shed door a crack so she could peek out. A man was standing at the back door of a small cottage, talking to a woman Kira assumed was his wife. He turned to walk toward the shed. Kira glanced round her hiding place. The shed was piled high with tools, gardening equipment, boxes and pieces of old furniture. There was nowhere she could conceal herself. She looked back out at the man. He was quite slim and not very tall. He wasn't one of those who had brought her and Elena to this place. She had to get past him to reach the road. She couldn't afford to be trapped in the shed. It was now or never. Gripping her rucksack in front of her, she burst out of the shed and charged at the man, roaring as loud as she could.

"What in the name o' the wee man...?" mumbled the startled man before Kira crashed into him, knocking him aside. He started to cry out, staggered backward and landed squarely on his backside. "Stop!" he blurted. "Come back here, you wee..."

But Kira was now sprinting along the road and, by the time he had dragged himself back to his feet and made it to the road himself, where his wife joined him, the young woman was nowhere to be seen.

"What was that all about?" asked the man's wife.

"Some lassie was in our shed," the man explained. "She ran off when she saw me coming."

"Did she steal anything?"

"Steal anything? Don't be daft. What's worth stealing in that shed? It's full o' rubbish. She'd have done us a favor taking some o' it away."

"What was she doing in there then?"

"I think she maybe slept there last night."

"In yon manky shed? Poor soul," said the woman. "If only she'd knocked on the door, I'd gladly have given her a bed."

"Aye but there's some no' as caring as us," the man said, turning back to the cottage, "and some that would do her harm. She was a lovely looking lassie. I've a mind to let yon Sergeant Macbeth in Lochdubh know she's sleeping rough. I'll phone him later."

"That's probably best," the woman said, linking her arm into his. "Now, how about a wee cup o' tea afore we start work?"

"That would be just braw," he said, brushing mud off the seat of his trousers as they walked up the path together. "She minded me o' you when we first met, Meg. A pretty young thing…"

"Give over, you old fool," Meg said, nudging him and giggling.

Kira lay out of sight in a field behind a drystone wall, listening until she was sure the couple had gone indoors. She then sat up, taking care to stay hidden, and took stock of her situation. She could see the inn some way down the road toward the beach where they had landed the previous evening. Now that it was light, she could also see that there were a few other small cottages like the one where she had slept scattered around the area. To get back to the inn where Elena was without being seen, she would have to double back, taking a route higher up the hillside where there were some bushes and trees for cover.

Then she had to get Elena away from that place...but where could they go? From what she had understood of what the couple had said, they sounded nice, but she and Elena couldn't immediately put their trust in complete strangers. They had to get as far from here as possible, but where should they start? She had heard the couple mention Sergeant Macbeth. What could he be? A border guard? A soldier? A policeman? They said he was in Lochdubh. Would that be a town, or a military base? Whatever it was, that seemed as good a place to start as any. Even if it was a military base, there might be a train station. Escaping from here by train seemed like a good idea, but they would need tickets. She took out the wallet, leaving the passports zipped safely in the inside pocket of her puffer jacket. The wallet contained a wad of £50 notes. She was used to using euros but knew that £50 would be worth more than €50. There was also a bank card and a credit card in the wallet. For now, at least, they had plenty of money.

It took her more than an hour to make her way back to the Loch Muir Inn where she hid herself in some bushes behind a wall and watched for any sign of Elena. Another hour passed before her friend appeared, carrying a basket of washing, which she began hanging on a clothesline in the inn's small back garden. Kira crept closer, making sure she couldn't be seen from any of the building's rear windows.

"Elena!" she breathed in the loudest whisper she dared. "It's me!"

Elena risked a glance toward her friend and gave a brief shake of her head. She carried on pegging the washing to the line and then began singing in Latvian to a tune she made up as she went along.

"The bearded one is watching me," she sang, "and listening, but he won't understand this. He seems nice but locks the door to my room at night, but I can force the window. Meet me here tonight when all is quiet."

Kira smiled. Elena was smart and, now that

she thought about it, she had quite a good singing voice, too!

Having polished off their breakfasts, Hamish dealt with some admin in the small office at the front of the police house while Davey settled in to the spare bedroom. They then set off to reacquaint Davey with Lochdubh and its environs. The weather was holding fair and they left the station without jackets, Davey wearing the modern, black, quarter-zip version of the police uniform shirt and Hamish in his preferred, traditional white. Despite repeated warnings from his commanding officer, Superintendent Daviot, Hamish refused to dress in black, claiming that the modern uniform made cops look like many things, from special forces binmen to ninja traffic wardens—but never proper police officers. Daviot, however, was based miles away in Strathbane and as long as he stayed there, the black shirts with which Hamish had been issued would stay in a drawer in his bedroom, factory fresh, and still sealed in their plastic wrapping.

Lugs and Sonsie joined them when they walked out of the station to head along the pavement by the seawall toward the center of Lochdubh. Lugs trotted along the pavement while Sonsie sashayed casually along the top of the low wall, but only until they saw that the tide was out and there were gulls to chase on the beach. They both then raced off for some fun.

"It's grand to be back walking along this path," Davey said, making a show of breathing in great lungfuls of fresh air.

"Better than Auld Reekie, any day," Hamish said. "The sea air by the loch ay gives you that braw whiff o' the freshest ozone."

"Two things to pick you up on there, Sergeant," Davey said, laughing. "Edinburgh's not as 'reekie' as it used to be—there's no smog from thousands of coal fires nowadays. The other thing is that the 'ozone' scent is actually dimethyl sulfide produced naturally by bacteria in the water that—"

"Enough o' your science malarkey!" Hamish smiled, holding up a hand to stop Davey in mid-sentence. "As far as the locals and the tourists are concerned, it's ozone and it's good for you."

"It's certainly good for you," Davey agreed, breathing deeply, "and way better than the air down south. Now, where are we headed first?"

"To the pub," Hamish said.

"Hang on a wee minute," Davey said, then laughed again. "I'm as keen to celebrate being back in Lochdubh as any man could be, but it's not yet nine in the morning and we're on duty."

"Aye, but we're no' going on a bender," Hamish assured him, "and you're no' the only recent newcomer in town. The auld pub has been refurbished, renamed and has a new landlord. We need to have a word wi' him and find out what he's like."

Lochdubh's only pub lay on the waterfront just beyond what one of Hamish's previous constables, Willie Lamont, proudly described as Lochdubh's finest Italian restaurant, the Napoli. Like the pub, the Napoli was the *only* Italian restaurant in the village, although that never seemed to trouble Willie when he was talking about the place he ran with his wife, Lucia. Approaching the

Napoli, Hamish and Davey spotted Willie walking toward them from the direction of the pub.

"Davey!" Willie gave the young officer a heartfelt greeting. "Good to see you, man! What are you doing back here in Lochdubh? I thought you were down in the capital robbing soldiers wi' the high and mighty!"

"Robbing soldiers...? Ah, right," Davey said, shaking Willie's hand and immediately recalling that Willie regularly got his words mixed up. "You mean rubbing shoulders... Well, I needed a bit more time on the frontline before I concentrated on the detective side."

"Have you been down to take a look at the pub, Willie?" Hamish asked.

"Aye, and I'm just after meeting the new landlord," Willie replied. "He's a big lad, Hamish. Looks like a tough nut, you know—and a bit intimate."

There was a short pause before Hamish spoke.

"Intimidating," he said, finally working out what Willie meant. "Well, I'm sure a landlord sometimes has to look a bit fierce to keep a rowdy crowd in order."

"Well, I wouldn't want to get rowdy wi' him around, that's for sure!" Willie said, laughing. "He's coming in for dinner tonight, so I need to get back and make sure everything's up to scratch."

Hamish sometimes missed having Willie around as his constable. The man was obsessed with cleaning and the police station had never looked so neat and tidy as when Willie had lived there. Davey was always willing to get stuck into the chores but Willie had turned housework into an art form. The two police officers walked on to the pub where an imposing figure was holding a ladder steady while another man balanced on it, attempting to hang a new pub sign—a stylized image of a highlander playing the bagpipes. Below the image was the pub's new name—THE PIPER.

"Good morning!" Hamish called, announcing their presence rather than risking startling the two men at work. It didn't do to surprise a man up a ladder.

The big man holding the ladder looked round, noted that two policemen had arrived, nodded and turned back to the ladder. Only when the man hanging the sign had finished and climbed down did he turn back to Hamish again.

"Sorry," he said bluntly, reaching out a massive paw to shake hands, "but Ronnie's a bit feared o' heights and my knees are no' up to climbing ladders these days. I'm Hector MacCrimmon, the new landlord."

"Good to meet you," Hamish said, introducing himself and Davey. "I thought we might drop by to see how you were settling in."

"We're near ready to open tomorrow night," said MacCrimmon. "Come ben and I'll show you what we've been doing wi' the place."

Hamish and Davey followed MacCrimmon in through the main entrance, Davey noting that the publican was tall enough to have to duck slightly to avoid cracking his head on the door frame. Davey was tall, and Hamish slightly taller, but both could make it through a standard doorway without having to stoop. Unlike Hamish, who was solidly built but long-limbed, Davey had a muscular physique earned through countless hours spent in a gym. Hector MacCrimmon, however, had the look of a man who was naturally powerful, even though he was now well into his sixties. The big man led them into the pub where they were impressed to find a freshly refurbished, immaculately clean main bar area. The wooden bar counter stretched across most of the back wall and was shining under multiple coats of glossy varnish. The floor, previously covered by a dark, patterned carpet that had been further darkened and patterned by years of spilt beer, was now bare wooden boards, sanded smooth and gleaming almost as deeply as the bar.

"I mind back in the bad old days when my boots used to stick to the manky carpet on the floor here!" Hamish said, laughing.

"Aye, we've made quite a few improvements," MacCrimmon said, looking round the bar with obvious pride.

"Is this you, Mr. MacCrimmon?" Davey asked, having crossed the room to examine some of the framed sporting photographs hanging on the newly painted white walls. The one he stopped beside showed a boxer standing in fighting pose.

"Aye, I fought a bit as an amateur when I

was younger," the landlord answered. "Had a few professional fights down south, too, afore I started having trouble wi' the knees."

"And the pipes behind the bar," Hamish said, pointing to a magnificent set of bagpipes on display next to the optics, "would they be yours? It would go wi' the name."

"They're mine, sure enough, and you're right to say they go wi' the name," said MacCrimmon, looking impressed that Hamish was knowledgeable enough to have made the connection. "MacCrimmons have been personal pipers to the chiefs o' Clan Macleod for ower four hundred and fifty years."

While Hamish and MacCrimmon chatted, Davey took the opportunity to study the older man. His hair was gray and thinning and his brow, like everything else about the man, was heavy and strong, making his dark eyes look as though they were perpetually half closed. Unlike most boxers Davey had ever met, MacCrimmon's nose was neither flattened across his face nor bent out of shape. Clearly not many of his opponents had managed to lay a glove on him.

"I'd offer you a drink, gentlemen, but you're both in uniform…" MacCrimmon said, frowning at Davey's black shirt, "…of sorts, and we're no' actually open until tomorrow."

"It's a shame you've missed most of the tourists," Hamish said. "The season's just about past."

"Well, I'll still be around when the tourists choose to come back," MacCrimmon said. "I'm here for the rest o' my days. This is my wee retirement project, so I'll see a good few tourist seasons come and go."

"Good to hear it," Hamish said. "The locals will be delighted to see the pub looking so grand."

"Aye, I've met a few and asked them in for the opening night," said MacCrimmon, "including Willie from the Italian. I'm in there for my supper tonight. Is it any good?"

"The food there is amazing," Davey said. "You'll eat well tonight, Mr. MacCrimmon."

"He was a bit funny, yon Willie," the publican said, with a slight frown of confusion. "Said we should be friends because we were the village intraparoors. What was he blethering about?"

"Sounds like he meant 'entrepreneurs,'" Hamish

said, smiling. "You'll get used to Willie mixing things up, but he's a good man. His wife, Lucia, is the chef. Her food is delicious."

"Aye, so I've heard," MacCrimmon said, nodding. "You'll both be coming along for the opening night o' the Piper, I hope?"

"We will," Hamish assured him. "I've seen the posters you've been putting up around the village. A piper's parade from the bridge, through the village, to the pub and the first drink free for anyone who joins the parade. You'll have a lot o' parade followers wi' that offer."

Hamish and Davey left the Piper, promising to be there for the opening, and headed off back to the police station to complete Davey's refamiliarization with the area by taking a tour up the coast to visit the farthest-flung corners of their patch. Davey didn't speak until they were well clear of the pub.

"I see what Willie meant about MacCrimmon being intimidating, Hamish. He's a big man, but there's something else bothering me about him. All those photographs on the walls were signed by top sports stars—football players, athletes,

tennis players, golfers, all sorts—and all dedicated to Hector. Seems he had some seriously
high-profile contacts down south."

"And down south is where the real money is,"
Hamish said, nodding in agreement. "So why
didn't he choose to open a bar down in Glasgow
or Edinburgh where his famous friends could
help to draw in customers? Why set himself up
in a place where he knows no one and no one
knows him? That's what I want to find out,
Davey—what exactly is Hector MacCrimmon
doing up here in Lochdubh?"

"Maybe he's here to get away from something
in the south," Davey suggested.

"Aye, and he'd no' be the only one, would he,
Davey?" Hamish looked Davey straight in the
eye and there was an awkward moment before
the young man swiftly turned away, quickening
his pace toward the police station.

Chapter Two

There is no sure foundation set on blood,
No certain life achieved by others' death.
William Shakespeare, *King John*
(1590s), Act 4 Scene 2

"I swear I'll murder the pair o' them when I get my hands on them! How did the lassie get out o' this place?" The dark-haired man slammed his fist down on the bar in the Loch Muir Inn.

"It wasn't my fault. I kept an eye on her during the day and locked her upstairs at night," the older, gray-bearded man said defensively. "Who'd have thought that wee slip o' a thing could force the window and climb all the way down, clinging on to the stonework? And she seemed right happy here, singing a wee song when she hung out the washing."

"You must be going soft in the heid!" snarled the dark-haired man. "They must both be out there together. Well, they'll no' have got far. They've no transport and it takes a day to walk out o' this neck o' the woods."

"They might be hitch-hiking."

"I drove down the only road that comes in here. There was no traffic and no sign o' them. We need to get out there now and find them afore they reach the main road up the glen."

"I'll need to be back by noon to open the bar."

"What the hell are you worrying about the bar for? Those two wee tarts know enough about our business to get us thrown in the jail! You'll no' have to worry about opening time then!"

"Aye, but some o' the regulars come a fair distance for their dram at the Loch Muir and I've been opening regular as clockwork every day except Sunday for the last twenty years. It would look right suspicious if I don't open—and we don't want anyone poking their noses in around here, now, do we?"

"You might be right. You'd better be back here in time to open. Maybe we'll need help out on the road, but I can sort that. From now on, when you're no' behind that bar, I want you out looking for those lassies. We need to find them, or I'll make sure you regret ever having clapped eyes on me!"

"You'll have no problem there," the older man muttered under his breath, watching the other march out of the bar. "I'm regretting that already!"

From an upstairs window in a small, white-washed cottage on the hillside looking down across the road and out over Loch Muir, Elena watched two vehicles heading in the direction of the main road.

"Two trucks," she said quietly in Latvian, remaining crouched out of sight of the drivers. "White one is from inn. Blue one went down toward inn earlier."

"They are looking for us," Kira said, sitting up in bed. "Don't worry, Elena, they can't see you from down on road."

"We need to go," Elena said, crossing the

room to perch on the single bed next to Kira's. "We need to get away from here."

"Not yet," Kira answered. "Here we are safe for now. Come downstairs. I will show you what I found last night."

The two women made their way down the narrow flight of stairs to the living room. It was a comfortably furnished room that stretched the whole width of the ground floor with a window at the front looking out toward the loch and another at the rear, facing the hill that rose steeply away from the small back garden. A mirror above the mantelpiece made the room look bigger and a small electric fire stood ready in the fireplace for use when the open fire was not lit. Kira turned on the fire to banish the morning chill. Both women were fully clothed and had been all night, having taken turns on guard, one resting, the other watching. No one had come anywhere near the cottage, but they had to be ready to run the instant anyone approached.

"I saw this last night." Kira pointed to a calendar on the wall opposite the fire and reached across a patterned sofa to retrieve it. Sitting on the sofa, the two girls flicked through the calendar's seasonal Highland images, looking at the dates printed beneath. "Look at dates marked here, Elena."

A yellow highlighter pen had been used to illuminate the dates for Saturday and Sunday every two weeks or so, with three entire weeks having been blocked out in July.

"This is weekend house," Kira said. "Holiday home used only two weekends each month and few weeks in the summer."

"That explains why there is no food in kitchen," Elena said. "No newspapers, no mess, like no one lives here."

"I think so," Kira went on, "but today is Friday and next dates marked are tomorrow and Sunday. We are safe here for a few hours. We can rest and eat."

"But kitchen is empty!"

"I found a small room beside kitchen," Kira said smiling. "There is a big freezer with plenty inside—and we have a micro-oven!"

"So we eat," Elena said, "then we go where cars have gone. Main road must be that way—other direction is to inn and beach only."

"Also there is hot water," Kira said, "and a shower in bathroom. I must wash, then I can prepare food while you shower, too. Who knows when we can do so again once we leave?"

Had a medieval knight or clan chieftain ridden his warhorse up the sweeping driveway of the Tommel Castle Hotel in Lochdubh, trotting through the avenue of rhododendrons, intent on conquering the fortress, he might have been dismayed for a moment by the building's solid stone turrets and battlements. Such defenses may have looked unassailable until his eyes dropped to rest upon the many large windows and the welcoming steps that rose gracefully to the glazed front door. Surely this place could never hope to repel even the weakest of assaults? Had some madman constructed a dangerously flawed castle? Not really. No marauding warrior had ever laid siege to the place, the "castle" having been built long after any occupants might have had to defend themselves against anyone more dangerous than an over-excited tourist.

A folly designed for a rich merchant who followed the trend when Queen Victoria and the coming of the railways in the nineteenth century made owning a grand Highland home the height of fashion, Tommel Castle's current owner, Colonel George Halburton-Smythe had turned the place into a hotel (at Hamish's suggestion) when he had fallen on hard times. A chain of ill-advised investments had seen the retired colonel's inherited fortune vanish horrifyingly quickly, although still not quite as quickly as the high-society friends he had cultivated. Struggling to entertain as lavishly, or as often, as he had once done left him with a precariously tentative toe-hold on the social ladder.

Nevertheless, as a hotel the building oozed elegance and grandeur, which, along with food served by another of Hamish's former constables, chef Freddy Ross, brought a new coterie of well-heeled visitors back time after time. The main difference between these guests and the colonel's old friends was, of course, that they paid for the privilege. On the estate, there was shooting and fishing available as well as walking in

the surrounding hills. From the bay window of
his study the colonel looked out over the estate,
which stretched from the shores of Loch Dubh,
over open meadows, through woodlands to the
shallow slopes of the mountains and on beyond
the summits. His study was on the first floor of
the private wing of the hotel occupied by himself,
his wife and, more often than not, his daughter,
Priscilla, whom he could now see standing by the
front steps chatting to the hotel's security manager, Silas Dunbar.

In the colonel's opinion, Dunbar was a solid,
conscientious chap. *Yes*, he thought to himself,
*Dunbar would have done well in the army. Not
officer material, of course, but he'd have made a
fine soldier under the right commanding officer.
Not like that lazy scoundrel Macbeth! Still, I've
managed to recruit two good men from Macbeth's
shambles of a police station.*

Like Freddy Ross and Willie Lamont, Silas
had also once been one of Hamish's constables,
although Priscilla and the hotel manager, Mr.
Johnson, along with Hamish, had far more to do
with finding the two former police officers jobs at

the hotel than had the colonel. Priscilla worked for an IT company in London but had recently found herself spending more time in Lochdubh than she did in the south of England. She and Mr. Johnson were the ones who actually ran the hotel, although the colonel truly believed he was in charge, taking a "strategic overview" while leaving his underlings to handle the tedious business side of things. He was convinced it would be some such trivia that Priscilla was discussing with young Dunbar. Then he saw Hamish and Davey walking up the driveway.

"It's that Forbes bugger!" the colonel muttered. "What the devil is he doing back here? I thought he'd gone for good!"

Hamish sighed as he watched Davey's reaction to seeing Priscilla. His shoulders straightened, settling ever so slightly further back, helping to puff out his chest a little. His chin lifted and his stride seemed more assured. He looked like a male pigeon with amorous intent and, in truth, Hamish thought, that probably wasn't too far off the mark. Not that he could blame the lad. Davey had fallen for Priscilla's charms when he had last been in Lochdubh and he wasn't the first to have done so. She was tall, strikingly beautiful with a glossy bell of blonde hair, and never looked anything less than drop-dead gorgeous, but Hamish knew the truth about her. He had been smitten by her just as badly as Davey. Worse, in fact—he'd become engaged to her and the whole village thought he'd gone mad when he called it all off. What no one else knew was that, behind the facade of charm and smarm, Priscilla was a cold fish, incapable of showing real love and affection to any man. She loved to be adored, but shared no love in return.

"Steady, Constable Forbes," he warned Davey, quietly. "Don't go getting yourself in ower your heid again...and mind your feet or you'll trip ower your tongue."

"Well, well, who do we have here?" Priscilla said, beaming a welcoming smile at Davey, which even Hamish judged to be genuine. "Nice to see you back home, Davey!"

"Och, I'm not sure this is really home, but..." Davey grinned sheepishly, stumbling over his words.

"Of course it is!" Silas said, shaking Davey's hand. "Hamish's constables never stray that far from Lochdubh! You're here, I'm here, Freddy's here and Dick Fraser only escaped as far as Braikie!"

"And then there was Dorothy," Priscilla said, staring straight at Hamish.

When PC Dorothy McIver had been assigned to Lochdubh, Hamish could hardly believe his luck. She was clever, brave, funny and the most beautiful woman he had ever seen. He had fallen head over heels in love and was the happiest man in Sutherland, the happiest man in Scotland, the happiest man ever to have walked the planet when he proposed to her and she said yes. His entire world fell apart when she was murdered by Glasgow gangsters on the morning of their wedding.

"Dorothy was the best of all of you," Hamish said, looking Priscilla straight in the eye.

"Aye, aye, she was that…" Silas said quickly, tiptoeing round the bomb that Priscilla had just dropped. "Hamish, come away in to the kitchen, say hello to Freddy and tell me what you think about the new locks we've got on the back door there."

The colonel, having maneuvered to the side of his bay window closest to the front door, had established a forward observation position behind the curtain.

"Where are they going?" he muttered under his breath, watching Hamish and Silas disappear into the building together. "Why have they left her alone with *him*?!"

"You've been keeping yourself in shape I see, Davey," Priscilla said, reaching out to squeeze a chunky Forbes bicep.

"Aye, I spent some time in the gym to get myself back in shape for some rugby down in Edinburgh," Davey said, relaxing a little, allowing himself a casual grin. "You've not changed at all, you know. You still look amazing."

Had the colonel been able to hear the sickly sweet swirl of compliments choking the air by his front door, as well as having seen his daughter tweak the over-muscled lout's arm, the boiling purple fury on his face may well have burst out of his eardrums. Was it not enough that Macbeth had the nerve to become engaged to his daughter? Was it not enough that he had brought disgrace on the Halburton-Smythe name by jilting her? Was it really necessary for her to take up with another callous, nincompoop of a policeman? Well, it wasn't going to happen. He'd make sure of that. He still knew people. Police Superintendent Daviot in Strathbane was a personal friend. He would know why that reprobate Forbes was back in Lochdubh. He'd be able to do something about the blighter!

"In the meantime," he growled to himself, storming over to his desk, "I still have some authority around here! I'm still the ranking officer in this castle!"

He snatched that day's copy of the *Scotsman* off his desk, tore it to shreds and flung it across the room.

"What have you been doing since you got back?" Priscilla asked Davey, motioning him to follow her toward the hotel's patio garden.

"We were out all day patrolling the district," Davey said, hoping it sounded more interesting than it actually had been. "Hamish wanted me to get used to the new Land Rover, so I did most of the driving. We'll be doing more of the same today."

He spotted a strange movement out of the corner of his eye and looked up to see strips of torn newspaper fluttering down the inside of a first-floor window.

"Then we had supper at the police station and a bit of an early night," Davey went on. "It had been a long day's driving for me. I set off to get here from Edinburgh in the middle of the night."

"I'm sure you coped," Priscilla said, raising an eyebrow. "You look like a man with...stamina."

"Aye, well...yes," Davey said with a nervous little laugh, "but it was still a long day. I have tonight off, though, and it's the opening of the new pub in the village. Will you be going to the parade?"

"Maybe not the parade," Priscilla answered. "I've got work to finish on an IT project, but I might make it to the pub later, just to see what it's like."

"Great!" said Davey. "I'll buy you a drink there."

They continued their stroll round the garden,

chatting and laughing, while the colonel stabbed at his phone, retrieving the personal number of Superintendent Daviot and making a call.

The colonel wasn't the only one peeking out from behind curtains. A few miles to the south, Kira was furtively watching the road from the front window of the cottage.

"White van has returned," she reported to Elena, who was curled in an armchair that matched the sofa, attempting to improve her English by reading a three-week-old copy of the *People's Friend* she had found in a magazine rack. "Blue truck must still be out looking for us."

"Women in Scotland must be obsessed with knitting," Elena said, closing the magazine and slipping it back into the rack on the floor by her chair. "So, we can go, but we must stay on road. Mountains are high and hillside is boggy. We have no boots or mountain clothes. We walk on road and watch out for blue truck. Hide when we see it."

"I think so," Kira agreed, turning away from

the window and looking round the room. "This is a nice house. We must leave everything as we found it."

Twenty minutes later, the two young women were on the road, walking with the calm waters of Loch Muir glistening in weak sunshine to their right and dense forests of alder and birch shrouding the hillsides all around, the birch leaves having turned a golden color but the alder remaining stubbornly green. Once beyond the loch, the road followed the river up Glen Muir and the only sounds were the breeze plucking autumn leaves from the trees and their own footsteps. It became clear that, on this road, they would probably hear the blue truck approaching before they could see it but that did little to mitigate the sinister beauty of the woodlands, from where it seemed like a thousand eyes could be watching them.

Here and there wide gaps in the trees opened out to reveal clusters of two or three buildings huddled together. They took great care when passing these cottages, scanning the premises for the blue truck before hurrying on. Eventually the road up the glen climbed to meet a wider main road where Kira and Elena were faced with a signposted choice—Lochdubh in one direction or Strathbane in the other. After studying the signpost for a while, Kira decided that Lochdubh, despite the strange spelling, sounded more like the place the man she had knocked over had mentioned when he had spoken about "Sergeant Macbeth."

At first, the bigger road seemed no busier than the one in Glen Muir but it was far more open, with drainage ditches either side and sheep grazing on moorland scattered with outcrops of rock that appeared more frequently as they walked. The mountains eventually began closing in on the road, which twisted through a series of bends. That made it more difficult for them to see very far ahead, or behind, although the air was still and quiet enough that they knew they would hear any vehicle approaching. There were now also blocks of densely planted, dark green spruce trees—ideal cover should they need to hide.

Before long they heard the sound of an engine

and leapt across the roadside ditch to hide in the trees. A silver car appeared from the direction in which they had been traveling, and cruised past their hiding place. No sooner had they got back on the road than a red car appeared behind them, the sound of the silver car having drowned out its engine. Kira and Elena froze. They were in plain sight and running off into the woods would look suspicious. They stood their ground at the edge of the road and the red car pulled up alongside them. The driver was a woman who looked to be in her forties, with dark curls of hair, friendly brown eyes and a gentle smile.

"Can I give you a lift, girls?" the woman asked.

Kira and Elena looked at each other and nodded.

"We would like to go to railway station," Kira said in her best English.

"The nearest station is in Lairg," the woman said. "That's about an hour's drive from here, but you're in luck. I have to pick up my son there in two hours and I need to drop my shopping off at home first. Why don't you hop in? We can have a cup of tea at my house and then set off for Lairg."

Kira and Elena looked at each other again.

"She seems nice," Kira said in Latvian.

"Blue truck will not see us in a car," Elena added. They nodded to each other again.

"Thank you," Kira said to the woman. "That would be very nice."

They climbed into the back of the car, where they sat with their rucksacks on their laps, ever vigilant for the blue truck. The woman introduced herself as Kathleen, then chatted merrily, glancing at her passengers in the rear-view mirror from time to time.

"How old your son?" Kira asked, trying to help keep the conversation going.

"He's twenty," Kathleen answered, "about the same age as you girls, I should think. He's spending a few days with me before settling back into university in Stirling. That's why I had to go shopping. You wouldn't believe how much he can eat!"

For the next twenty minutes, Kathleen kept up a stream of stories about her son and how much he was enjoying university. They drove past the road that led down to Lochdubh and headed on up the coast toward Scourie for a few miles. Kathleen then pulled off the road through a gateway onto a track that led to a modern, two-story house sitting in an overgrown garden on a hillside, with a clutch of other similar houses not too far distant. She jumped out of the car and called for Kira and Elena to follow.

"Come away in now," she said. "We don't have too long."

She unlocked the front door and led them into a bright living room with a large window facing the front garden. There was a television, a sofa, two armchairs, a sideboard, and a print of a fishing boat painting above a mantelpiece, beneath which was a wood-burning stove. The house felt cold, slightly damp and when Kathleen dumped her car keys on the coffee table in front of the sofa, the light from the big window picked up a plume of disturbed dust.

"Sit down, now, both of you," Kathleen said, smiling and waving at the sofa. "I'll just pop into the kitchen to put the kettle on."

Sitting on the sofa Kira and Elena exchanged another glance. Both looked worried.

"Food for her son is still in car," Elena whispered. "House is cold and dirty—not ready for her beloved son's visit. Something is not right here."

"You are right," Kira agreed. "Look around…" She glanced at the window sill, the mantelpiece and a sparsely populated bookcase. "A loving mother who has no photos of her son? Maybe there is no shopping in car. Elena, you can drive, I cannot. Take car keys, quickly."

Elena snatched the keys from the table, stuffing them into the pocket of her jacket. No sooner had they done so than they heard Kathleen coming back into the room, talking on her phone.

"Aye, no worries," Kathleen said. "I've got the pair o' them here. They're no' going anywhere now."

Kira and Elena looked round to see Kathleen place her phone on the sideboard, then grip the forestock of the shotgun she was pointing at them to steady her aim.

"Stay right where you are," she said, a cold calmness in her voice. "Do what I say now, girls, or, believe me, I will shoot you."

The two young women watched Kathleen move carefully round to stand by the fireplace in front of them, with just the coffee table between them, the twin barrels of the shotgun trained on them every moment.

"The passports and the wallet," Kathleen said. "On the wee table. Slowly now. My finger's on the trigger."

Kira and Elena reached into their jackets, Elena placing her passport on the table, Kira her passport and the stolen wallet.

"Now all we have to do is wait, so—" Kathleen began, then her phone rang on the sideboard. She looked toward it and in that instant of distraction, Kira launched herself across the coffee table, knocking it over and shoving the shotgun barrel aside. She pinned Kathleen back against the mantelpiece.

"Elena! Start car now! Go!" Kira yelled, wrestling Kathleen, still clinging to the shotgun, to the floor. Elena leapt to her feet and dashed out the front door to the car. She started the engine then saw a flash from the cottage window and heard what sounded like a thunderclap. Kira immediately appeared, bounding out the door toward the car.

"Drive!" she yelled, tumbling into the passenger seat. "Go, now!"

With the engine racing, Elena fought to keep the car on the narrow track down to the main road, the tires screeching when they hit the tarmac.

"What happened?" Elena asked once they were speeding down the road.

"Never mind," Kira answered. She looked down at her left hand and was horrified to see smears of blood. The smears were joined by another falling drip and she realized the blood was her own. Her nose was bleeding. "Just drive," she said, pulling a tissue from her pocket to dab her nose. "Just drive. Fast. Far away."

The Braikie Lions Cycle Club celebrated the coming of spring each year with their biggest and most prestigious event—the Assynt Century Race. First run in 1990, the race was named for the club's centenary and for the fact that the road-race circuit was 100 miles long. Following a route from Braikie into Glen Oykel, then east to Lairg and Loch Shin before taking the A838 "Five Lochs" road northwest to Laxford Bridge, the racers then sped down to the coast at Scourie and home to Braikie via Kylesku. No one had ever bothered to measure the route—everyone simply knew it was 100 miles.

Kevin McCready had come third in the race last year and second this year. Next spring he was determined to win. That's why he was out cycling the course, training hard, determined to ride the roads as many times as he could before the winter weather set in. If he was honest with himself, he enjoyed setting off from Braikie and returning home almost as much as he did the ride through the mountains. If he was really honest with himself, he'd have admitted that he loved the way he saw people admiring him in his skintight Lycra cycling gear. He liked to show off how fit he was. Had anyone else been honest with him, they'd have pointed out how ridiculous they thought a slightly podgy, middle-aged man looked riding a skinny wee bike in an outfit three sizes too small for him. Fortunately for all concerned, no one ever chose to be quite that honest.

Kevin was cruising down the A894 on the descent to Loch Assynt with the cliffs and crags leading to the Quinag summit on his right and the gentler slopes climbing southeast to the foothills of Ben More Assynt on his left. This was a fast stretch of road for him with lots of bends to glide through, but the chance to make good progress with minimal effort. Now that the tourist traffic had subsided, there were also very few other road users to hinder him. He leaned into one left-hander and hit the pedals to power down a straight section when a red car came from behind, flying past him so close that the slipstream made him wobble, he hit a pothole he would otherwise have avoided, and was flung off the bike and off the road into a soggy ditch.

In the moment it took him to recover his senses and get to his feet he heard the blare of a car horn and looked down the road ahead to see the red car being dealt a glancing blow by a blue pickup truck coming up the hill. The blue truck skidded to a halt, the red car swerving out of control and lurching into the same ditch from which he had just extricated himself.

Two young women emerged from the red car and ran off, disappearing from sight away from the road behind a tangle of gorse amid a rocky maze of boulders. A man jumped out of the truck, looking back to where the women had gone.

"Bloody maniacs!" Kevin yelled.

The man, still some fifty yards away, looked from the seemingly deserted moorland where the women had vanished, up to where Kevin stood, then climbed back into his truck.

Kevin hauled his bike onto the road. The front wheel was buckled. Maybe the man would give him a lift. The blue truck, however, picked up speed as it approached him, then swept past, the driver sparing not even a glance for the stranded cyclist.

Kevin reached for his phone in the zip pocket at the back of his shorts but the truck was gone round the bend before he could photograph it. As was so often the case in the mountains, he also had no phone signal. He hoisted his bike onto his shoulder and walked down to where the car lay in the ditch, noting the airbags that had deployed and deflated, hanging limply from the dashboard like morning-after party balloons.

"Are you there?" he shouted toward the rocks. "I know you're not hurt. I saw you running. What are you playing at? Show yourselves." He might as well have been talking to his broken front wheel. No one appeared and there was no sound bar a few ticks and creaks from the ditched car and the breeze sweeping the hillsides. Kevin swore and started walking down toward the loch and Inchnadamph, the pedal grip cleats on his cycling shoes clacking noisily on the road with every step.

Hamish and Davey arrived at the start of the parade dressed as anyone who recalled Davey's previous posting to Lochdubh would remember them. That, given no one in Lochdubh ever forgets the faces of the local police officers whose salaries they pay through their hard won and reluctantly relinquished taxes, meant just about everyone. Having been a detective constable at that time, the two officers had regularly been seen in the village, Hamish in uniform and Davey in a casual shirt and trousers. So it was again this evening, Hamish having decided that Davey should have the night off, mainly because Claire's shift pattern meant that he would want the following night off.

There were no more than a dozen locals gathered at the car park near the bridge on the edge of the village but once Hector, resplendent in a kilt of the predominantly blue MacCrimmon tartan, fired up his pipes, belting out a rousing rendition of "Scotland the Brave" followed by "Highland Laddie," it seemed that every house or cottage the parade passed disgorged one or two who merrily marched along.

"He's like 'The Pied Piper,'" Davey said, laughing. "People can't resist the call of the pipes."

"Aye, right," said Hamish with a wry smile. "I'm thinking it's more like the call o' the free drink."

By the time they reached the Piper, the parade followers had turned into a small crowd who packed out the pub. Once the initial rush to the bar had subsided, Hamish and Davey stepped forward to be served. Hamish accepted a lime juice with soda and Davey a pint of lager.

"I thought you'd have a good few takers for your free-drink offer, Mr. MacCrimmon," Hamish said.

"First one's free but no' the second," Hector replied with barely a smile.

"Still, it's a great turnout for your opening night," Davey commented.

"Aye, no' bad," Hector said nodding, "but there's one I'd like to have seen who's no' here."

"Who might that be?" Hamish asked.

"A good friend who promised to come along," Hector said. "Mick—Michael Gallagher. I saw him a few days ago but haven't seen hide nor hair o' him since. He's no' answered his phone or any messages I've sent. Seems like he's just vanished."

"That's a shame," Davey said. "Why would he not be here?"

"You'd best ask them," Hector said, polishing a glass and nodding to a table where two men and a woman sat together. "They'll ken where he is and if anything's happened to him, they'll ken exactly what."

"Who are they?" Hamish asked. "I don't think I know them."

"The woman is Mick's wife, Shona," Hector explained. "The men are her father and brother—Andrew and James MacDougall."

The sinister tone in Hector's voice made Hamish decide that it was time he got to know the Mac-Dougalls. More than a few faces turned to watch him and Davey approach their table. There was plenty of loud chat and laughter in the bar, but when two police officers walked up to a bunch sitting on their own, there was always the chance something interesting might happen. The Mac-Dougalls sat, the men with glasses of whisky, the woman with what looked like a gin-and-tonic she was drinking through a straw, making no acknowledgment of the police officers' presence.

"Good evening," Hamish said. "I'm Sergeant Hamish Macbeth and this is Constable Forbes."

"Aye, we ken fine who you are," said Andrew, the older MacDougall, without looking up, "and we'll be obliged if you just leave us alone."

"I'd be happy to," Hamish said, "but I was wondering why Mr. Gallagher isn't here tonight. I understand he was expected."

"We've no idea where he is," James said. "He disappeared a few days back. Maybe he's gone off on his fishing boat. We thought we might catch up wi' him in here tonight."

"A few days?" Davey asked. "How many days, Mr. MacDougall?"

"What does it matter to you?" James replied.

"Well, we'd expect a wife to report her husband missing as soon as he didn't come home," Hamish said. "We take missing persons reports very seriously, even more so after forty-eight hours have passed."

Shona Gallagher sat with her head bowed, staring down at her drink. She hadn't looked up to acknowledge the two police officers and her long brown hair hung forward like curtains, hiding most of her face.

"He might have had some kind of accident, Mrs. Gallagher," Davey suggested. "He could be lost or having trouble with his boat. We might have to mount a search."

"If he's lost, I'll no' search for him," she said, without looking up. "If he's gone, I'll no' miss him and if he's deid, I'll no' mourn him."

"That's no' usually how we hear a wife talk about a missing husband," Hamish said.

"He was no husband to me," she said. "He's no' a real man, just a nasty wee shite."

"You must have been fond of him at one time," Davey said, "given that you actually married him."

Finally she looked up and swept her hair back from the left side of her face. Her cheek was bruised and swollen to the extent that her eye was almost closed. The left side of her mouth was swollen and cut. Dark blue and red bruising clouded her jaw.

"If I'd known he was capable o' this, I would never have gone near him, let alone marry the swine," she said, "but he could be a real charmer when he wanted to be, you know? When we first met he was full o' smiles and gentle as a lamb. A year or so later, it all started to change and I never knew what sort o' mood he'd be in when he came in off the boat. This is no' the first time

I've had to hide my face. Yon rings he wears make a fine mess, do they no'?"

"We shouldn't have come here, lass," said her father. "Let me take you away home now."

"No!" the woman snapped. "If he's coming in here to see his old pal Hector, then I want to stand in front o' him, right there by yon shiny new bar, and show everybody what sort o' a monster he really is!"

"And when you do, Mrs. Gallagher," Hamish said, "I'll be right here to slap the cuffs on him."

"Aye, maybe we weren't so interested in tracking him down before," Davey said, clearly shocked by the appalling bruising to the woman's face, "but he's a wanted man now. Even if he's not in here tonight, we'll find him all right."

"No' if we get to him first," said the younger man.

"You're no' to lay a hand on him, James!" said Mrs. Gallagher. "I'm no' having you or Dad getting into any trouble on his account. You leave him be."

"We'll see about that," her brother replied, tossing back his whisky.

"You should listen to your sister, Mr. Mac-Dougall," Hamish said. "You have to leave this to us."

"We'll need you to make a statement, Mrs. Gallagher," Davey said.

"A statement?" Shona Gallagher gave a snort of derision, took a sip through her straw and then looked straight at Davey. "Aye, here's a statement for you. Michael Gallagher is the most disgusting creature ever to crawl on the face of the Earth and I wish he was deid so I could spit on his grave!"

"That's enough now, lass," her father said, putting his arm around his daughter, who sobbed into his shoulder. "Don't go upsetting yourself all over again. You're safe wi' us now."

If the fact that the two police officers had walked up to the MacDougalls' table hadn't drawn enough attention from the rest of the Piper's customers, Shona's outburst left every face in the bar turned toward them, the babble of conversation settling to a deathly hush. Then came a familiar drone and Hector appeared in the middle of the room, his pipes under his arm and the strains of "The Green Hills of Tyrol" filling the air, instantly accompanied by hand clapping, foot stomping and the assembled voices singing "A Scottish Soldier."

"James," Hamish said, loud enough to cut through the din as far as James MacDougall. He nodded toward the door, leading Davey and James out into the car park away from the noise. "Leave Gallagher to us," he said once they gathered together. "That's twice I've told you. I count that as fair warning. Don't try taking the law into your own hands, or I'll be locking you up along wi' Gallagher."

"That would suit me just fine!" James snarled. "Lock me in a cell wi' the bastard and only one o' us will be walking out again! You ken he had another woman on the go as well? Aye, he was cheating on Shona and if she ever said a word out o' place, he beat the living daylights out o' her! Well, he'll never lift a hand to her again once I catch up wi' him. I'll give him a taste o' his own medicine and some more besides! He's a deid man walking!"

Chapter Three

Temper is a weapon that we hold by the blade.

> J. M. Barrie, *The Little Minister* (1891)

"Cut the hard-man crap, James!" Hamish said. "We'll find Gallagher, but we need your help. Have you got a photo? Any kind o' family photo will do as long as it shows his face."

"Aye, I must have something on my phone, I suppose," James said, avoiding Hamish's stern glare and staring at his shoes.

"Send it to me," Hamish said, handing James a card, "and persuade your sister to make a statement. If she needs a couple o' days to calm down, that's fine, but let's do it sooner rather than later. We need a statement from her so we can charge him. We can take the statement at your place if that suits her best."

"I'll speak to her," James said. "She'll do your statement. She'll be happy for you to nick Gallagher, even if she doesn't want me and Dad going after him. No' that she'll be able to stop us. Dad is boiling mad about what he's done."

"Any idea where he might have gone?" Davey asked. "Will he still be in the area?"

"Who knows?" James answered. "He has yon fishing boat o' his but he can't handle a boat that size on his own."

"Do you know any o' his crew?" asked Hamish.

"No, he never let us near the boat," James explained. "He was operating the boat afore he met Shona and we know nothing about it."

"And Shona bides wi' you and your dad, now, does she?" Hamish asked.

"She does. We don't want her back in the house she shared wi' Gallagher."

"Good," Hamish said. "We'll want to take a look at her house."

"I'll send you the address," James said, grabbing his phone and punching a short message to the number on Hamish's card. "It's on the road to Braikie. You can go there whenever you like. If the back door's locked, there's a key on the lintel."

" '*If* the back door's locked'?" Davey sounded incredulous. "You mean it might not be? You're not too bothered about basic security, then?"

"It's no' my place, okay? And you don't come from round here, pal," James said, rounding on Davey. "You lot down south might no' trust your neighbors, but things are different up here, right? So maybe you should keep your smart comments to yourself!"

"Take it easy, James," Davey said, raising his hands slightly in a calming gesture. "I didn't mean anything by that. I'm on your side, remember?"

"Aye, right!" James growled. "I'll keep telling myself you're on our side. It's easy to forget wi' you lot!"

James stomped off back into the pub, Davey watching him go before turning to Hamish, who was standing with his arms folded and an amused smile on his face.

"Touchy, isn't he?" Davey said.

"He's putting on a bit o' an act if you ask me. I think he knows far more about Gallagher than he's saying, but what you called the 'touchy' bit was genuine. Even if his sister hadn't just been beaten up, he'd have been every bit as 'touchy' wi' you," Hamish replied. "You know why, don't you?"

Davey sighed and nodded, shoving his hands into his pockets.

"Because I'm an outsider—a prat from the south who just told a local man outside his local pub how he should be living."

"Right first time!" Hamish said, laughing. "Take a look along the street at the houses and cottages there. It's no' dark yet, so none o' the back doors will be locked, even though most o' the householders are likely enjoying a dram or two in the Piper right now. In fact, most o' the front doors are probably unlocked as well, even the ones right on the street. Come night time, when they're all off to bed, half o' them will still no' bother locking the back door, because they've never done so their whole lives. People have a different attitude to things like that here. So what

73

does someone like you, an outsider, have to do to win over the locals?"

"Maybe," Davey said, with a resigned smile, "I should try not to be such a southern prat."

"That would be a good start," Hamish agreed, giving Davey a good-natured slap on the shoulder. "I know what it's like, Davey. I've been here for years, but I wasn't born in Lochdubh, so there's plenty here still think o' me as an outsider, too—and always will!"

Davey perked up a little at that, and a little more at the sight of Priscilla walking toward them, casually dressed in jeans and a waxed jacket but with her hair and makeup, as always, immaculate.

"Aha!" she said with a flirtatious smile. "My two favorite policemen. I was hoping I would bump into you before I got to the pub. It never seems quite right to me for a lady to walk into a pub on her own."

"Then you must allow me to buy you a drink," Davey said, offering her his arm, through which she immediately linked her own. "Are you coming back in, Hamish?"

"No, Davey, I'm away back to the station," Hamish said. "It's your night off tonight, remember? I'm off tomorrow."

"A hot date with your lovely wee paramedic?" Priscilla asked.

"Aye, that's the plan all right," Hamish nodded, forcing a smile when he realized he'd sounded like a reluctant participant in the "hot date." The truth was, Claire was pressing him to discuss taking a holiday together. She wanted to go somewhere hot and sunny, as she put it, "to get some warmth in my bones afore winter sets in." Hamish knew he should be showing more enthusiasm for the idea, but he never faced the thought of leaving Lochdubh for any length of time with anything less than mild dread. He pushed the thought of planning the holiday out of his mind.

"See you buy Shona and the MacDougalls a drink, Davey," he said. "You need to mend some bridges there."

Hamish arrived home to a rapturous welcome from Lugs and Sonsie, both of whom were waiting in the kitchen to be fed. Clearly wondering where Davey was, Lugs stuck his head out the back door for a moment, looking for his friend. Sonsie made a point of not doing so. Once he had filled his pets' bowls, Hamish made himself a cup of coffee and sat at the kitchen table.

"Well, you two seem happy enough wi' your supper," he said to a chorus of munching accompanied by the tinkle of collar identity tags against metal food bowls. "Now I've to decide what I'm going to eat."

That, as it turned out, was as close to an evening meal as he was to get. His personal radio suddenly squawked and the familiar voice of a long-time friend in Strathbane filled the kitchen.

"Strathbane to Sergeant Macbeth," came the voice.

"Good evening, Alex," Hamish said, plucking the radio from his belt. "What's up?"

"We've had a cyclist come into the station, Hamish," Alex explained. "He says a red car forced him into a ditch on the Strathbane road near the junction wi' the road down to

Lochdubh. The car was then forced into the ditch itself by a blue pickup. The driver o' the pickup left the scene and two lassies legged it from the red car. He wasn't able to give any description other than they were wearing jeans and hoods. He thought they were girls on account of the way they moved."

"I'll go take a look," Hamish said. "I'll let you know what I find when I get there, Alex."

It took Hamish just a few minutes to cruise through the village in his Land Rover and cross the ancient stone humpbacked bridge over the River Anstey, freshly rebuilt after the storm-swollen river had used a floating tree trunk as a battering ram to try to demolish it. Hamish gave a slight shudder at the memory of that night. The collapsing bridge had almost taken him with it. The road snaked up through a stretch of forest onto more open moorland before reaching the junction with the A894. He spotted the red car in the distance almost straight away and scanned the surrounding landscape as best he could while approaching the crashed vehicle. He saw no sign of anyone, let alone the two young women who had reportedly abandoned the crashed car. Pulling up alongside, he switched on his blue flashing lights as a hazard warning for any other road users who might come along, then got out to take a look around.

There was certainly no sign of the car's occupants and a brief search of the vehicle revealed nothing untoward inside save for a smear of what might have been blood on the passenger's seat. The bloodstain, if that's what it was, was not significant enough to suggest any serious injury and there was nothing else to give him the impression that anyone had been badly hurt in the crash. The ditch wasn't deep enough for the car to have sustained much damage and he reckoned it was probably still driveable, although it would need to be winched back onto the road. He climbed into the Land Rover to call Strathbane.

"Hamish here, Alex," he said. "No sign o' anyone up here by the car. It's no' badly damaged but it will need a tow truck to get it out and transport it down to Strathbane. Looks like it might have been nicked by joyriders and abandoned when they crashed it. I've just run the license plate through the computer in my car and it's come up wi' two addresses for the registered keeper, Kathleen Tait. One is in Strathbane but the other is only a bit further up the road to Scourie, so I'll pay her a visit."

Having set up portable hazard lights at the scene, a few traffic cones and some blue-and-white police tape, Hamish set off to find Kathleen Tait's house.

All seemed quiet when he pulled onto the short track leading up to the house, then he noticed the front door was standing open. He parked his car and walked warily toward the house. Something felt decidedly wrong.

"Hello?" he called, nudging the front door further open and leaning inside. "Police! Anyone home?"

He walked up the short hall and turned left to stand in the open doorway of the front room. The place was a mess. An armchair was tipped on its side, a gaping hole in its upholstery, the stuffing strewn in all directions. A coffee table lay broken in the fireplace and a picture of fishing boats hung at a crazy angle above the mantel-piece. Hamish sniffed the air, instantly recognizing the smell of a recently discharged shotgun. He stepped back from the room, looked out the front door toward his car and up the hall to where a staircase led to the upper floor. There was no one making a break for the road and no one coming at him from the stairs. Standing very still, he listened hard, but could hear no signs of movement. He stole a quick glance back into the front room, looking round toward the rear of the house where he saw a shotgun lying on the floor and, in the far corner, a woman sitting slumped against the wall with her chin on her chest.

In two strides he covered the distance to where the woman lay.

"Can you hear me?" he called, touching her neck and then her wrist to feel for a pulse. "Can you..."

When he tried to see if she was breathing, the woman slid sideways, looking up at him from the floor with wide, lifeless, brown eyes. For a moment, Hamish couldn't tear himself away from the death stare. Then he remembered the shotgun and turned to pick it up, breaking the barrel to eject the two spent cartridges. He had no idea if anyone else was in the house but if he wasn't alone, he didn't want anyone getting hold of the shotgun. There was no dodging a double-barrelled blast in such an enclosed space. He tucked the unloaded gun beneath the sofa, out of sight. Moving stealthily to the kitchen, he saw a handbag sitting on one of the worktops, but nowhere that anyone could hide. He then checked the rest of the small house. Upstairs there was a bathroom and two bedrooms. One bedroom had a double bed, a wardrobe and a dressing table, the other was completely bare, with just a few battered, empty cardboard boxes on the floor. He found no one. A quick look around outside confirmed the property was deserted.

Hamish walked back into the sitting room and examined the dead woman. There was no blood or gaping wound, so she hadn't been shot. Neither was there any blood splattered around the room, the armchair being the only apparent victim claimed by the shotgun. The woman did, however, have massive bruising to the side of her face, possibly a broken jaw, but that hadn't been what had killed her. Livid weals showing as finger marks around her throat told him she had been strangled. He sighed. She would surely have been terrified and frantic, fighting for her life when she died. The thought made Hamish angry. What kind of monster would do this? And who was this poor woman? Was this Kathleen Tait?

He remembered the handbag in the kitchen and sifted through it, looking for identification, finding a driving license. The photograph on the license card matched the dead woman. This was, indeed, Kathleen Tait. Tucking the license back into the handbag, he walked outside, sat in his car for a second or two to gather his thoughts, then picked up the radio.

"Alex, it's Hamish," he said. "I've found Kathleen Tait. She's been murdered."

It was the sort of evening that somehow seemed warmer than it had been during the day, even when the daylight had faded and darkness was starting to deepen the shadows lurking in the mountains and forests around Lochdubh. Perhaps they simply felt warm because they had been overheating in the crowded pub but, whatever the reason, Davey and Priscilla enjoyed a casual stroll from the Piper to the front door of the Tommel Castle Hotel.

"You haven't said how long you'll be here for," Priscilla said as they lingered at the foot of the steps.

"Neither have you," Davey replied. "I thought your job was down in London."

"It is, I suppose," Priscilla agreed, "but I find myself spending more of my time up here nowadays. The internet connection is good enough for me to work from here. It's also more pleasant up here in the summer. London can get a bit too hot and overcrowded with tourists. Plus, I enjoy helping out with the running of the hotel during the busy months. The visitors here aren't quite so…frantic as in London. So what about you? Are you planning to stay this time?"

"For a while," Davey said. "It will do me good to work in uniform for the time being."

"Priscilla!" The colonel stood in the hotel doorway. "What are you doing out here skulking around with this scoundrel?"

"Really, Father!" Priscilla scowled at him. "Davey was kind enough to walk me home from the village, that's all!"

"Well, I'll bet that's not all he had in mind!" thundered the colonel. "I've been doing some checking on your 'Davey' and he appears to have left a trail of licentious scandal in his wake worthy of the front pages of the gutter press!"

"Really, Davey?" Priscilla's eyes widened, the angry expression to which she had treated her father turning to a bemused smile. "I always thought you were interesting, but now you're becoming positively fascinating. What have you been up to?"

"Not anything nearly as bad as your father's making out," Davey burbled. "I mean, quite bad… but not totally…" His phone rang loudly and he plucked it from his pocket, pressing the answer button when he saw that it was Hamish calling.

"Davey," Hamish said, "your night off's cancelled. There's been a murder. How much have you had to drink?"

"Only two or three pints," Davey responded.

"Too much to drive," Hamish noted. "Get yourself back to the station, get yourself some coffee and man the phone there. I'll talk to you once you're back."

"Aye, okay, I'm on my way," Davey said, then turned to Priscilla. "I'm sorry but I have to get back to the station."

Then he sprinted off down the driveway before Priscilla or her father could say another word.

Hamish battled the settling darkness, using his car headlights and his torch to help him see what he was doing, stretching yards of police tape around the house where he had found Kathleen Tait's body. From the sparse scattering of homes in the vicinity, a few of the boldest residents trudged along the main road to find out what was going on. No one would admit to having seen or heard anything unusual, although

Hamish found it hard to believe that no one had heard the shotgun blast. Even though the gun had gone off indoors, the sound of both barrels being fired would have been like a bomb going off in this quiet spot.

Before long, he saw the flashing blue lights and headlight beams of a convoy of cars speeding up the road from Strathbane. Two uniformed constables were the first to arrive and he assigned one to guard the gate, sending the other to keep an eye on the rear of the property. A couple of paramedics were next on the scene, taking only moments to confirm that the victim was most definitely dead. The next car disgorged Hamish's old friend, Detective Chief Inspector Jimmy Anderson.

"What's the story here, Hamish?" Jimmy asked, walking briskly up the track. Hamish took a couple of hurried steps to keep up. Jimmy had worked hard to recover from the injuries he had sustained in a car crash and, with Hamish having helped cover the fact that Jimmy had been drinking and driving, the chief inspector had worked equally hard to beat his problem with alcohol. As a result, he now seemed to have more energy than ever before.

"The dead woman is Kathleen Tait," Hamish explained. "Looks to me like she's been strangled but somebody also pulled both triggers on a double-barrelled shotgun in there. Blew an armchair to pieces."

"Was she maybe shooting at her attacker?"

"I doubt it. It's no' too big a room, there's no blood and wi' a gun like that, you'd no' miss."

"Suspects?"

They stopped by the front door and Hamish gave Jimmy a quizzical look. The older man returned his stare, with just a trace of a smile broaching his lined, fox-like features.

"I ken fine you've no' had time to launch any kind o' inquiry," Jimmy said, "and I'm no' expecting you to do the job o' a whole murder squad, but something brought you up here to Tait's house and you've had plenty o' time to think about it."

"Tait's car was taken, and it crashed off the road," Hamish explained. "A witness said it looked like it was forced into the ditch by a blue pickup. You'll have passed the crashed car on the way here. Two women were seen running from the car, so we need to find them. The other driver sped off. Apart from that, I know nothing about Kathleen Tait."

"Well, we'd better start finding out about her, and fast," Jimmy said.

"You seem in an awfy rush ower this one, Jimmy," Hamish said. "What's the hurry?"

"The woman's name has been ringing alarm bells down in Strathbane," Jimmy explained, "but nobody kens why, no' even Daviot. All we have is a link to another name, Michael Gallagher. Do you ken him?"

"Aye, yon's a familiar name, all right," Hamish said, taking off his cap and ruffling his shock of red hair. "I met his wife, Shona, and her family, Andrew and James MacDougall, earlier tonight. According to them, he beat her up a few days ago. He's now gone missing. The family's after his blood, and they know he had another woman. If you've linked him to Kathleen Tait, then I'm guessing she could be the other woman."

"So we've got the two women who stole her car, Gallagher's wife, the MacDougalls and Gallagher himself—a violent man—as suspects," Jimmy said, shaking his head. "I've never had so many suspects in such a short space o' time. We need to interview them all—that means finding the mystery women and Gallagher, pronto!"

"Aye, I think it would be a good idea to find Gallagher afore James MacDougall does, otherwise, we might just turn up another body."

"That would not be good," Jimmy said, pulling on some latex gloves. "Bide here while I take a wee look afore the forensics lads get in."

Jimmy spent only a minute surveying the murder scene before he was back on the doorstep with Hamish, where they were joined by two forensics officers, the senior of whom was a woman in her fifties, most definitely not one of Jimmy's "lads." She tucked her blonde curls into the hood of her white forensic suit and looked up at Hamish.

"You discovered the body, Sergeant Macbeth," she said—a statement rather than a question.

"I did," said Hamish.

"Did you touch anything when you were in there?" she asked.

"I touched the body to check for signs of life," Hamish replied, sounding slightly defensive. "I touched the shotgun to make sure it was unloaded and safe. My priority then was to look for any other injured people, or the culprit, on the premises, so you'll find a fair few o' my fingerprints about the place. I didn't fancy being jumped by a killer while I was fiddling wi' a pair o' gloves and…"

"It's okay, Sergeant," the woman said. "We know what it's like. As long as it was only you and the paramedics in there, that's fine."

"She's all right, that one," Jimmy said, watching the two white-clad figures disappear into the house. "Right, Hamish, I need you on this straight away. I'll have my lads chasing down any contacts they can find and we'll go to Tait's place in Strathbane, but you know your patch better than anyone. If Gallagher's still alive, we have to find him!"

"Aye, okay, Jimmy," Hamish said, slowly, trying to calm his friend. "I've an address for the house he lived in wi' Shona, but I doubt he'll go there. The MacDougalls will be watching for him doing that. He also has a fishing boat, so we can find out where that is. What's so desperate about this, though? What's all this about alarm bells in Strathbane?"

"I'm no' sure," Jimmy replied, "but there's talk that they're sending in a team from Glasgow. If that happens, then we'll lose control o' what's happening on our own doorstep. I don't like it. It's all a bit...fishy."

"Aye...fishy," Hamish agreed, walking back down the track with Jimmy. "I'll tell you what else seems a bit fishy to me, Jimmy—Davey Forbes in uniform and in my police station."

"What are you on about?" Jimmy said, looking slightly uncomfortable.

"Well, if I mind right, you're his godfather, are you no'?" Hamish said. "And his father's a high-ranking officer down south—your old pal from police training college in Tulliallan. Davey should be set on a solid police career in Edinburgh, so what's he doing back here?"

"I've no time for that right now," Jimmy said,

pulling his phone from his pocket and dialing a number. "The laddie will tell you all about it himself when he's good and ready. Just don't go listening to a load o' auld wives' tales in the meantime. Now get some o' that lot," he pointed to a group of uniformed officers standing by the gate, "going house-to-house along the length o' this road to see if anybody saw anything. Give me the address and I'll get a couple o' my lads to check out Gallagher's house, but now I need to get back to Strathbane."

Hamish sent the officers, who were joined by a couple of Jimmy's detectives, to start knocking on doors as far north as Kylestrome and as far south as Inchnadamph. He visited the very closest houses himself. At the first house, the door was answered by a man he recognized as one of the locals who had come to the gate earlier.

"Good evening, sir," Hamish said. "I believe I saw you earlier, didn't I? As you know, we're investigating an incident at yon—"

"We've been in all day and we've seen nothing and heard nothing," said the man.

"Are you sure?" Hamish asked, looking over the man's shoulder where he could see what was clearly the man's wife in a texting frenzy, her forefinger flitting across the keypad, no doubt transmitting lurid details of everything she hadn't seen and hadn't heard to everyone she knew. "You're the closest house. Did you know your neighbor well?"

"Never met her," said the man. "Now, if you'll excuse me, it's getting late."

The reaction at the next house was markedly different. It was a low, two-room cottage with a sizable patch of hillside in front of it enclosed by the most impressive drystone wall Hamish had ever seen. It ran over the undulations in the terrain like a snake, maintaining a uniform height and a smooth ridge of coping stones. The cottage door was opened by a small man with a flushed red face, a halo of wiry gray hair and a bushy gray beard. His whole head looked like a pimple on a scouring pad. His tired old eyes peered out from behind wild gray eyebrows and he wore a black waistcoat over a black shirt and black trousers.

"Thank the Lord!" he said, probably the most

enthusiastic greeting Hamish had ever received on a house-to-house inquiry. "I thought you'd never get here. Come away ben."

Hamish followed the little man into a spartan living room, where the furniture consisted of two cushionless dark-wood chairs and a wooden table in front of a small, peat fire. The room was lit by a single electric bulb hanging from the ceiling and nestled in a plain white lightshade. On a side table sat a Bible, its black cover bearing a simple white cross. The only other adornments to the room were a birdwatching book along with a pair of binoculars on the front window ledge and, on the chimney breast, a black-framed quotation:

For every house is built by someone, but the builder of all things is God.

Hebrews 3:4

The flagstone floor boasted no rug to warm or brighten its cold darkness and the walls were painted white, bare but for a plain wooden crucifix and another quotation in a frame identical to that over the fireplace.

The rich rule over the poor, and the borrower is slave to the lender.

Proverbs 22:7

"Can I offer you some tea, Sergeant?" asked the old man, indicating the tin teapot, two white mugs and a milk jug on the table.

"That would be most welcome," Hamish said gratefully, and they sat down to talk, the man introducing himself only as Shepherd and explaining that he lived a simple life alone here in his cottage. When Hamish asked if he had seen or heard anything unusual at the nearby house, Shepherd took a sharp breath and tensed.

"There is everything unusual about yon house!" he declared, reaching out for his Bible and clutching it to his chest. "It is not a place for decent, God-fearing people! It is a wicked house—a house of sin!"

"Are you saying you think it's a brothel?" Hamish asked. "I don't believe it's being used for anything like—"

"A man visits regularly. He brings with him the strong drink!" Shepherd declared, holding his Bible

95

aloft. "'Wine is a mocker, strong drink is raging: and whosoever is deceived thereby is not wise! '"

"A fine sentiment," Hamish agreed and then, gently encouraging Shepherd to tell him more, he said: "I take it this man comes in a car of some sort."

"That he does," Shepherd confirmed. "A blue pickup truck..." And to Hamish's delight Shepherd recited the license plate number.

"What about the woman who lives there?" Hamish asked. "What do you know about her?"

"The harlot!" Shepherd breathed. "She brings women to stay there in her red car. Her red car! Hidden in her red car as though concealed beneath the scarlet cloak of the Whore of Babylon!"

"Did she bring two young women to her house today?" asked Hamish.

"Aye, there were two today. I saw them," Shepherd said, nodding toward the binoculars by the window, then staring into the fire "They were rare beauties both. I saw them arrive. So beautiful..." He raised his Bible high again. "'Walk in the Spirit, and you shall not fulfill the lust of the flesh! '"

"But they didn't stay long, did they?" Hamish ventured.

"They did not. One ran out to the car, then there was a flash at the house window and a bang. Even wi' my fading ears I could hear yon sound. The sound o' a gun—the sound o' death! Then the other one ran out and they drove away, very fast. I fear for the souls of those poor lovely lassies. They killed the harlot, didn't they?"

"That's what I'm trying to find out, Shepherd," Hamish said softly. "There's been a lot of excitement for you today, I suppose, with me and all these other police cars arriving."

"Aye, and the blue truck," Shepherd said, sounding tired.

"The blue truck was here today, too?"

"It was. It arrived just after the lassies left. The man didn't stay long. He loaded some boxes into his truck—that would be the demon drink again! Then he left in a hurry, just like the lassies. I will pray for their souls."

He bowed his head, closing his eyes as though in silent prayer, and Hamish sat quietly until he heard Shepherd's regular breathing turn to delicate snoring. He then discreetly saw himself out. Scarcely pausing to nod a greeting to the constable guarding the gate to the crime scene, he hurried to his car and entered the license plate number of the blue truck on his computer. When he saw the results that came up on the screen he immediately reached for his phone and called Jimmy.

"Jimmy, it's Hamish. Michael Gallagher was right here at the murder scene earlier today. It was his truck that forced Tait's car off the road."

Hamish eventually made it back to Lochdubh in the early hours of the morning, having waited for a new shift of officers to arrive from Strathbane to guard the crime scene. Davey was waiting for him and had even made a cottage pie, Hamish devouring the portion Davey had left for him before collapsing into bed. He was woken after a brief few hours' sleep by the smell of coffee and frying bacon.

"I know you ate when you came in," Davey said, stirring the bacon in the frying pan, closely watched by Lugs, "but a bacon roll never goes amiss in the morning, does it?"

"It never does," Hamish agreed, sauntering into the kitchen wearing an old T-shirt over his uniform trousers. "You fully up to speed wi' everything to do wi' the murder last night? Anything come in to you here?"

"A call from the outward-bound activity center came in early this morning," Davey said, stuffing two large breakfast baps with bacon. "They're only open at weekends now the summer season's over, and the staff reported the break-in when they arrived to open up."

"We can pay them a visit later if we have time," Hamish said, thanking Davey for his bacon roll. "Anything else?"

"We had a call last night from a bloke down in Glenmuir who said a woman had been sleeping rough in his shed. He only got a brief look at her but said she looked really young and he was worried she might be some sort of runaway."

"Really?" Hamish said through a mouthful of bacon, then his brow furrowed slightly into a thoughtful frown. "Does that now mean we're looking for three lassies on the run? And Glen-muir...funny place for any kind o' runaway to end up."

Once Hamish had shaved and dressed, he and Davey walked out to the Land Rover, Hamish opening the tailgate to let Lugs and Sonsie spring inside, both pets delighted, as always, to be taking a trip in the car. The two police officers were about to climb in the front when they spotted the formidable figures of Nessie and Jessie Currie standing by the police station's garden wall, staring at them. The Currie twins had been old ladies for as long as Hamish could remember, yet never seemed either to grow any older or to change at all. Both wore identical tweed hats, pink-framed spectacles, beige camel-hair coats fastened up to the neck and sensible brown leather shoes with matching handbags. Had he been challenged to spot anything remotely unusual about them, he might have guessed that their tightly permed gray hair possibly looked a little more mauve than normal. The grim expressions on their faces were certainly as foreboding as always.

"We have to report a serious crime!" announced one of the twins without any greeting or pre-amble. Hamish immediately knew this was Nessie—the only way he had ever been able to tell them apart was that Nessie always spoke first.

"Serious crime!" Jessie, Hamish knew, always spoke second and had the irritating habit of repeating the last words her sister had said.

"Good morning, ladies," Hamish said, giving them a broad smile, "and what would that crime be now?"

"Grand larceny!" Nessie announced boldly. "A federal offense!"

"Federal offense!"

"I think you've been watching those American TV cop shows again, haven't you?" Hamish said. "We don't actually have what you might call a 'federal offense' in Scotland."

"Nevertheless, Sergeant Macbeth," Nessie said, adopting a defiant stance, setting her feet slightly apart and folding her hands in front of her, moves which were immediately copied by her sister, "we have suffered a grievous injustice!"

"Grievous injustice!"

"Can you tell us exactly what's happened?" Davey asked.

"We were both up extra early this morning to bake a fresh batch of our special shortbread," Nessie explained.

"Special shortbread," confirmed her sister.

"When we left it on the kitchen window ledge to cool," Nessie went on, "some filthy thief came and stole the lot!"

"Stole the lot!"

"That's a disgraceful crime, right enough," Davey said, with a serious expression. "I remember your shortbread and it was the best I've ever tasted."

"We remember you, too," Nessie conceded. "We heard you were back."

"Heard you were back."

"I thought I might see you at the parade last night," Davey said. "The Piper played some fine old Scottish tunes. 'A Scottish Soldier' went down well in the pub."

"The pub is no place for ladies," Nessie said, "and that song is not old and not Scottish!"

"Not Scottish!"

"What do you mean?" Hamish asked.

"The words were written in the late fifties by the singer Andy Stewart," Nessie said.

"Andy Stewart."

"And the tune comes from Rossini's opera, *William Tell*," Nessie informed them.

"*William Tell*."

"If that's no' your sort o' music, ladies," Hamish asked, his curiosity getting the better of him, "what do you like?"

"In church we prefer psalms to hymns," Nessie said, "and at home in the morning we like Bach, in the afternoon we like Debussy and in the evening—"

"Led Zeppelin!" Jessie squealed, interrupting her sister who looked at her, horrified, tutting and shaking her head. Hamish promised they would look into the theft of the shortbread and the twins marched off along the pavement, heels clicking in unison, although not quite loud enough to cover what Hamish convinced himself was the sound of Jessie humming "Stairway to Heaven."

"We're not really going to spend time investigating the great Lochdubh shortbread heist, are we?" Davey asked, leaning on the car.

103

"We've other things to do," Hamish said, handing him the car keys. "You can drive."

Davey looked delighted to be taking the wheel again but Hamish had a puzzled expression when climbing into the passenger seat.

"On the other hand," he said, "it strikes me as weird that anyone would steal the Curries' shortbread."

"Why?" asked Davey. "It's the most delicious—"

"Aye, I'll agree wi' you there," Hamish cut in, "but nobody around here would thieve it because the Curries give the stuff away to anyone who wants it. So who's been prowling round the back o' the Currie twins' house? And if they've been in the Curries' back garden, who else had been paid an unwelcome visit? Has anyone else had something taken? In short—who stole the shortie?"

Chapter Four

Fortune! if thou'll but gie me still
Hale breeks, a scone, an' Whisky gill
Robert Burns, "Scotch
Drink" (1785)

Hamish decided that their first port of call that day would be at the house Shona Gallagher had shared with her husband in Braikie. Letting Davey drive gave Hamish the opportunity to appreciate familiar views upon which, from the passenger seat, he could let his eyes linger a little longer than usual. The sun was making welcome, if fleeting, appearances from behind high, lazy clouds blowing in off the Atlantic, sending cloud shadows creeping across the cnoc and lochan landscape of Assynt.

The cnoc—glacier-molded outcrops of three

105

billion-year-old rock that had an almost magical ability to transform from a dull, light brown to a sparkling light gray depending on how the sun hit them—were scattered throughout the glens and lower slopes of the mountains. Higher up, layers of red sandstone, newer rock that had formed over the bedrock perhaps only a billion years ago and had not been scraped away by the long departed valley glaciers, dominated the mountain crags and cliffs.

The hillsides, although mostly devoid of trees save for in wind-sheltered gulleys, were a lush green, their carpets of vegetation enjoying a vigorous burst of life in sporadic autumn rain prior to the coming of dark winter days. The rain had also swollen the lochans, the scores of small lochs scattered across the countryside. Most of these had never been named and many wouldn't even be counted among Scotland's 31,000 official lochs, but the anonymous pools shone proudly nevertheless, like precious jewels set in the swathes of green wetland.

To Hamish, this part of the country had always been beautifully wild and untamed, a fiercely independent land, although the mountainsides he was admiring all actually belonged to someone. The local Assynt Crofters' Trust had been created to purchase some of the land in order to give the crofters the opportunity to shake off the burden of tenancy, while other estates were owned by conservancy trusts dedicated to maintaining the natural beauty of the area. Along with Coigach to the south, the region had been designated the Assynt-Coigach National Scenic Area, one of forty such areas in Scotland, affording it government protection from damaging development or unsuitable exploitation.

Some of Assynt, like much of the Scottish Highlands, remained in private ownership. Hamish sighed, looking off into the distance toward Ben More Assynt, which he knew stood on the Vestey family's Assynt Estate. It had always seemed strange to him that, even though it was in a protected area, an estate which included such a magnificent mountain could be owned by a super-rich family organization headed by a baron who lived 650 miles away in London. That, however, was the way things had been for centuries.

"What's on your mind?" Davey asked.

"Nothing, really," Hamish said, quietly, "and everything…everything you can see. All o' this…" He waved his hand at the windscreen, indicating the panorama of mountain, glen and sky that had opened in front of them just as Davey had turned a corner. "If I owned a patch o' this—a patch that stretched as far as you could see—I would never want to live in a big city hundreds o' miles away."

"Why would you?" Davey said, recognizing the melancholy of a strange brand of homesickness that he had seen afflict Hamish and other Highlanders, even when they were in the heart of their own territory. "This is your home, Hamish. This is the country you love, and I can well understand why. It's beautiful."

"Aye, it is that," Hamish agreed. "Don't worry, Davey. I've just got too much birling round in my heid. Let's get to Braikie and check out that house."

They sank into silence, Davey concentrating on the road which had now started its descent into the first patches of forest on the outskirts of Braikie.

The house was a modern building in a small cul-de-sac of houses that all looked pretty much the same. The white, harled walls were topped with slate roofs and short driveways sat to the side of small front gardens. Hamish saw a net curtain twitch in the nearest neighbor's house the moment the Land Rover drew up.

Jimmy Anderson's detectives had already visited the house and found nothing of interest but Hamish, with Jimmy's blessing, was determined to take a look himself. DCI Anderson was well aware that Hamish's local knowledge could mean a picture on the wall or a book on a shelf might trigger a connection in the big Highlander's brain that would never be made by anyone else.

The front door and back doors were locked but, as James MacDougall had promised, a key to the back door rested, out of sight, on the lintel. The back door led directly into the kitchen which, like the rest of the house, appeared to have been left in a reasonably tidy state by the previous police visitors. Some search teams, Hamish knew from bitter experience, were quite capable of leaving turmoil in their wake with drawers tipped out and mattresses turfed asunder. More often than not, it had fallen to him to make peace with the local householder and, to mend relationships, even help to tidy up. Thankfully, it didn't look like that would be necessary on this occasion.

They found three bedrooms upstairs where some of Shona's clothes, but very few of her husband's, were hung and tucked away in wardrobes and drawers. Once downstairs again, Hamish and Davey stood in the large lounge-cum-dining room. It was an open, light-filled room that stretched from the front window to the full-height glass garden doors at the rear.

"What strikes you about this place, Davey?" Hamish asked, looking round at the modern furniture, the TV and the gas "flame-effect" fire in the fireplace.

"I'm not really sure," Davey said. "It's a nice house, but it doesn't feel right. It seems sort of... flat."

"Aye, it's like no one's actually put their mark on the place," Hamish agreed. "It's a bit like

Tait's house. There's no special wee touches—no family photographs."

"Shona took them," came a voice from the kitchen doorway and they turned to see Andrew MacDougall standing there. "She took all the nice things that meant something to her and binned the rest."

"Mr. MacDougall," Hamish said. "We weren't expecting to find you here."

"Nor I you," Andrew replied. "The other police came and went last night. We thought we'd seen the back o' you."

"We wanted to take a look for ourselves," Davey explained. "We were hoping we might find something to help us track down Gallagher."

"If there was anything here to tell where that bastard is," Andrew assured them, "James and I would have found it and him by now."

Andrew MacDougall wasn't a big man— his son, James, carried more bulk—but he had the tough, wiry look of a man who has known physical labor all his life and his eyes blazed with hatred when he talked about Gallagher.

"How is Shona?" Hamish asked.

"Better than she was yesterday," Andrew said. "No' as good as she'll be tomorrow. Her bruises will heal but those are no' the only wounds that animal has left her with." He tapped a finger on his forehead. "She hasn't left the house, save for that visit to the pub where we thought we might find Gallagher. The nightmares, the trauma, the fear, the dark thoughts about that man will likely never leave her. That's what he has to pay for, and we'll make sure he does."

"I warned James, Mr. MacDougall," Hamish said, gravely, "and the same applies to you. We'll deal wi' Gallagher. If you try taking any kind o' vengeance, I'll have no choice but to arrest you, too. I can't have you taking the law into your own hands. Believe me, we'll get him for you."

"Out of interest, Mr. MacDougall," Davey asked, "how did you know we were here?"

"We live no' too far away," Andrew replied. "I was a builder afore I retired, and I built all the houses in this development. Some o' the people who bought them are still friends. The neighbors next door here keep us informed o' comings and goings."

"When did Shona and Gallagher move in here?" asked Hamish.

"Just ower two years back when they got married," Andrew said. "She'd known him barely six months."

"How did they meet?" Davey asked.

"She worked in a bank here in Braikie," Andrew explained. "He used to be in there regularly, paying in cash. Said he bought and sold things. Claimed to have spent years working down south."

"Did you have any idea what he was like?" Davey asked. "Did you know anything of him before he started seeing Shona?"

"I'd never seen hide nor hair o' him before," Andrew said. "Neither had anyone we ken. Claimed he was born and raised ower near Rogart, but we ken nobody round yon neck o' the woods."

"I was brought up around there, too," said Hamish, frowning, trying to remember a Gallagher family. "Can't say I mind o' any Gallaghers."

"That doesn't surprise me," said Andrew. "We never met any o' his family, nor any o' his friends.

He said his parents had passed and he was an only child. He insisted on a wedding at the registry office in Braikie. It's no' what I would have wished for my only daughter, but she was besotted wi' him and wanted only to please him.

"In the end, there was nobody at the wedding from his side. He asked James to be his best man. We tried our hardest to make it a grand day for Shona, but it wasn't like a proper wedding. The whole thing broke my poor wife's heart."

"Is Mrs. MacDougall with Shona now?" Davey asked.

"My wife died wi' the cancer not six months after the wedding," Andrew said.

"I'm sorry to hear that, Mr. MacDougall," Davey said, looking slightly awkward.

"You weren't to know, laddie," Andrew admonished him. "Maybe if she'd been able to hang on a bit longer, Shona would have come to us sooner. Maybe she'd have let us know what a monster her husband had turned out to be. She was ay close wi' her mother."

"We'll still be wanting a statement from Shona, Mr. MacDougall," Davey said.

"Come by later this afternoon," Andrew said, and gave his address. "Shona and I will be there."

"There's some fine auld malt whisky on the shelf here," Hamish said, aiming to change the conversation by examining a cabinet in the corner of the room. "A couple o' rare and expensive bottles. Too rich for my pocket."

"Gallagher's," grunted Andrew. "The one thing he was never short o' was money. I'll no' take the bottles, but I can't bring myself to pour them away, either. They're yours if you want them."

"Och, that's awful generous o' you, Mr. MacDougall," Hamish thanked him, "but that wouldn't be right and could get me the sack, so I'll have to decline."

"I see," Andrew said, looking Hamish in the eye, impressed with his apparent ethics and honesty, but not entirely convinced. "Well, if there's a bottle missing after I'm gone, I'll no' mind and no one else will ever know. You'll keep us informed about Gallagher, won't you, Sergeant Macbeth?"

"I will," Hamish promised, aware that a deal was being struck, "as long as you do the same for me."

"You have my word," Andrew said, reaching out to shake hands with both Hamish and Davey. "Now I'll get back to Shona. Lock up properly afore you leave, please."

Hamish and Davey went through the house in greater detail, even fetching a collapsible ladder from the car in order to search the attic, but they found nothing to point them in Gallagher's direction. Then, just before they stepped out the back door, Hamish paused for a moment.

"On you go to the car, Davey," he said. "I'll be with you in a wee minute. I'll lock up."

As good as his word, Hamish climbed into the passenger seat almost as soon as Davey had clipped on his seatbelt. Once they were out of the cul-de-sac, Hamish reached inside his shirt to retrieve a bottle of twenty-one-year-old Glenfiddich from where he had hidden it from the neighbors' prying eyes.

"Hamish, you never did!" Davey said, taken aback, eyes flitting from the road ahead to the bottle and back again. "That's right out of order!"

"Well now, Davey, I'm thinking it was too good an offer to turn down," Hamish said, grinning. "Who's to know, after all? This will be our wee secret." Then, his grin relaxing into a teasing smile as he looked pointedly at Davey, he added, "And you're good at keeping secrets, aren't you, Davey?"

Davey gave a short breath, shook his head in resignation and concentrated on the road. He headed back in the direction of the route they had taken through the high pass, but had not gone far before Hamish asked him to make a slight detour.

"We're no' too pressed for time, Davey," he said, checking his watch. "Take the next on the left and we can go by the hospital. It's only a few minutes away."

"You mean Claire might be only a few minutes away," Davey said, giving Hamish a sideways look and an impish grin. "You haven't seen her for two whole days. You must be missing her."

"Aye, well." Hamish shifted uncomfortably, as though he'd suddenly found he was sitting on a back pocket full of loose change. "We send the odd text message and…" Hamish glowered at Davey. "Just drive, Constable!"

"As you will, Sergeant," Davey said, laughing. "Would you like the blue lights and siren?"

Hamish tutted, relaxed his frown and allowed himself a smile. He had been a little worried that he might have upset Davey with his comment about "keeping secrets" but, even if he had, the lad had bounced right back. His good humor was never far from the surface and it was infectious. Whatever the problem down south that had returned him to Lochdubh, Hamish was glad to have him back. He plucked his phone from a pocket and sent Claire a text. When they pulled into the hospital car park, she was waiting with three beakers of coffee.

"It's just from the machine inside," she said, almost by way of apology, "but it keeps us going."

She handed one of the coffees to Hamish and stood on tiptoe to kiss him on the cheek. Davey's phone rang and he excused himself, leaving Hamish and Claire to take a seat on the car park's low brick wall.

"Are you on a break right now?" Hamish asked.

"No' really," Claire said. "We've just brought

in an old man who had a fall but they're so short staffed here there's no doctor for us to hand him over to, so we're responsible for him until somebody's available. Charlie's wi' the poor man."

"That means you're no' available for any other call-outs," Hamish said, sipping his coffee.

"Aye, but the system is what it is—we're stuck wi' it," said Claire with a shrug. "I heard about you finding the dead woman up by Scourie."

"Yon was a bad one," Hamish said, sighing and shaking his head. "There's two young lassies out there on the run somewhere that we need to find."

"Are they the killers?"

"Can't be sure o' that," Hamish replied, "but they're in some kind o' trouble."

He explained about the two young women having abandoned the victim's car after being forced off the road. Claire looked into his hazel eyes, reached out a hand and gently stroked the side of his face.

"You look tired, Hamish," she said. "You need to take some time out from all o' this."

"Aye…the holiday…well, I've been thinking about that and—"

"No' a holiday, you daftie," she said, snuggling into his shoulder. "Don't worry about that right now. It's Saturday, remember? We're out to dinner tonight. We can have a few hours just to relax by ourselves."

"Of course," Hamish said, wrapping his arm around her. "How could I forget?"

They finished their coffees, Claire returning to work and Davey joining Hamish in the Land Rover. They drove out of Braikie up onto the high ground and then south toward Glenmuir, turning onto the road that followed the river down to Loch Muir about half an hour later. The house where the potential runaway had been reported was a neat, whitewashed stone cottage separated from the road only by a narrow front garden. As they pulled off the road into the track at the side of the cottage, Hamish could see well-tended vegetable plots on a tract of land behind the house, with a few chickens patrolling an enclosure outside their coop, one of a handful of outbuildings. Farther up the hill, a small flock of sheep was grazing.

They were greeted by a smiling, middle-aged woman when they stepped out of the car. She introduced herself as Meg Soutar and then called for her husband.

"Billy! Sergeant Macbeth's here!" She waved and pointed to the two police officers when Billy appeared from one of the sheds. "Come ben, lads, and I'll get the kettle on."

She led them into a kitchen warmed by a peat-burning cooking stove. The work surfaces were busy with the clutter of baking and food preparation, a mess for which Meg apologized profusely.

"We'll use the electric," she said, filling an electric kettle at the sink and motioning them to take a seat at the wooden table by the window. "A kettle takes ages to boil on the stove. Make yourselves at home, lads."

Billy Soutar then appeared and hurried to the sink to wash his hands before greeting Hamish and Davey with a handshake.

"We don't get many visitors," he said, smiling, "but we're ay happy to see anyone as does drop by."

"Even your uninvited guest in the shed?" Hamish asked.

"Aye, that was strange," Billy said. "I mean, what was a lassie like that doing sleeping in a shed away out here?"

"What do you mean, 'a lassie like that'?" asked Davey.

"A real good-looker—Billy's no' stopped talking about how lovely she was!" Meg said laughing, watching her husband's face flush with embarrassment. "He was right smitten—says she was a proper belter!"

"I was not smitten," Billy said, laughing at his own embarrassment. "She certainly took me by surprise, though!"

"Can you give us any more of a description?" Hamish asked.

"She had on a green jacket, one o' yon puffy things, and jeans," Billy said. "Very straight, long dark hair and big dark eyes. That's about all I can tell you."

"Do you think anyone else might have seen her?" Davey asked. "You don't have many neighbors here in Glenmuir."

"We like to be self-sufficient here," Meg answered, "but we're no' anti-social. There are more cottages than you might think scattered along the glen and we see some o' the neighbors from time to time."

"Do you meet up down at the inn?" Hamish asked.

"No' really," said Billy. "Yon's an odd place. It has plenty o' custom for a couple o' months during the summer when folk on holiday camp in the field near the beach."

"The rest o' the year there's ay a few cars go by most days," Meg added. "They come from farther up the glen and goodness knows where else, but it's no' a very welcoming place if you were to walk in there."

"It's like a drinkers' club," Billy explained. "Any time we went down there, Meg was the only woman in the bar and the men all just sit there talking among themselves."

"Our nearest neighbor is Mrs. Roberts just a

wee bit farther down the glen," Meg said. "She's here every other weekend since her husband died. I saw her car pass early this morning, so she'll be there. Maybe she's seen something o' Billy's wee beauty—or maybe we just had a visit from a fairy princess!"

They laughed, chatted and finished their tea before Hamish and Davey drove a couple of minutes down the glen to find Mrs. Roberts's house. Like the Soutars' home, it was a tidy, whitewashed cottage with a slate roof and, on approaching, they could see an elderly woman with short gray hair standing at the front door, waving at their car.

"Good afternoon," Hamish said, stepping out of the car. "I'm Sergeant Macbeth and this is Constable Forbes. Would you be Mrs. Roberts?"

"I am," she said, then looked into Hamish's face, smiled for an instant and looked away again, "and I'm glad to see you, gentlemen."

"Why's that, Mrs. Roberts?" Davey asked, walking round the car.

"Because I appear to have had a couple of secret guests," said Mrs. Roberts. "Come ben and take a look."

The two policemen seemed to create a crowd in the small hallway, feeling conspicuously large when Mrs. Roberts, who barely came up to their armpits, bustled through to her kitchen. Hamish and Davey walked into the room and separated, standing either side of the door like two enormous Police Scotland bookends.

"Just look," she said, standing by the sink and waving her hand at some crockery in the draining rack. "What do you think of that?"

Hamish and Davey stared at the sink, then looked at each other and shrugged.

"Honestly, Hamish Macbeth," said Mrs. Roberts with a playful smile, "you used to be the best at the observation games we played—Look and Learn."

"Look and Learn...Mrs. Roberts..." Hamish looked carefully at the woman standing in front of him, then his eyes widened, his head jerked backward ever so slightly and his face was infused with what Davey could only think was a kind of boyish excitement. He looked...gleeful. "Mrs. Roberts! Davey—it's Mrs. Roberts!"

"Aye, Hamish," Davey said, "I know who this lady is..."

"No, you don't," Hamish said, grinning. "Mrs. Roberts was my teacher when I first went to school!"

"And he's still the same," Mrs. Roberts said, chuckling. "Tallest bairn in class and hair like a red squirrel. Now, pay attention, Macbeth. This is how I found my kitchen—what do you see?"

"Okay," Hamish said, calming himself and studying the sink. "Two plates, two mugs, two knives, two forks. Two people have eaten here and...done their washing up?"

"Correct," said Mrs. Roberts. "Now we're getting somewhere. I should say that nothing has been stolen—I wouldn't be quite so relaxed if I'd been robbed. Upstairs the two single beds in my spare room have been slept in and then made up neatly. The shower has been used and then wiped down."

"So two very tidy people were here when you were away," Hamish said.

"I didn't see any sign of the front door or this back door being forced, Mrs. Roberts," Davey said, immediately cursing himself for sounding too keen to be better than Hamish at Look and

Learn. "Is this how they got in?" He used a pencil from his pocket to lift a loose latch on a fanlight window by the back door.

"Yes, I've been meaning to have that fixed," she admitted. "It must have been someone small and slim—none of us would fit through that wee window and I always keep my doors locked. Whoever came in probably unlocked the door to let the other one in. When they eventually left, they pulled this door closed," she nodded at the back door, "and locked behind them—and there's more."

Mrs. Roberts strode forward, placing her hands lightly on the arms of the two big policemen as though to stop them collapsing in on her before she could make it through the doorway to the hall. In the living room, she stood in the middle of the floor watching Hamish and Davey enter.

"Now what do you notice?" she asked, sniffing the air.

Hamish and Davey followed her cue and had a sniff.

"There's a very slight charred scent," Hamish

said, "like you get when dust is burnt off when you switch on an electric fire that's no' been used in a while."

"And then there's this," Mrs. Roberts said, pointing to the mantelpiece where there was a framed photograph of her with a taller, bald man standing in London's Trafalgar Square. Pushed beneath the frame was a £50 note. "They left me some money. Please, do take a seat, gentlemen."

Mrs. Roberts offered them tea which, even though they had enjoyed the same, with home-made cookies, in the Soutars' kitchen, they were happy to accept (with chocolate biscuits). Davey had lost track of the number of times Hamish had explained that declining Highland hospitality is every bit as insulting as calling a Highlander's kilt a skirt, calling his dog a haggis or telling him that Sean Connery wasn't the best James Bond.

"So you're saying that two people broke in here, without doing any real damage and stole nothing," Davey said in summary. "They had something to eat and washed up afterward; slept in the beds then remade them; had a shower, then wiped it all down; used your electric fire, then left you fifty quid and locked the door on their way out."

"Not the kind of burglary you're used to dealing with, I should think," Mrs. Roberts said.

"Certainly not," Davey said. "Burglars can make a real mess. I can't imagine any burglars we've ever dealt with who would tidy up after themselves. Men like that want to get in and out as quickly as possible and that generally means leaving complete chaos in their wake."

"You say men," Mrs. Roberts pointed out, "but surely not all housebreakers are men?"

"Ninety percent of burglaries are committed by men," Davey said, "and three-quarters of those men are under forty years of age."

"Davey's good on statistics and suchlike," Hamish said, "but the plain truth is a man breaking into your house will rip the place apart looking for cash or valuables. None o' them would ever dream o' leaving everything spic and span. We're no' dealing wi' two men here, Davey—it's two women."

"The two from the car?" Davey suggested.

"That would be my bet," Hamish agreed.

"What about the one from the shed?" Davey asked.

"My goodness," Mrs. Roberts laughed. "You two sound like you've got girls stashed all over the place!"

"It's no' what it sounds, Mrs. Roberts," Hamish said, laughing. "We've just got a few faces we need to track down. Tell me, do you still live ower in Rogart?"

"For the time being," said the old teacher, "but I'm thinking of moving here permanently. My husband and I put a lot of work into this place. The plan was to retire here but I'm afraid he didn't quite make it."

"I'm sorry for your loss, Mrs. Roberts," Hamish said. "Would that be your husband in yon photo?" He pointed to the picture on the mantelpiece.

"Yes," Mrs. Roberts replied. "We took a trip to London to see our daughter and our grandchildren last year. You know, everyone at the school always thought you'd move away one day,

Hamish. We thought you'd outgrow Sutherland as fast as you outgrew your old school shorts!"

"No' me, Mrs. Roberts," Hamish said. "I've seen plenty o' places and I've cousins all ower the country—all ower the world—but Sutherland's my home. This is where I belong. You must feel much the same yourself."

"Yes, you're right, although I wasn't born up here," Mrs. Roberts explained, "but I've lived here for more than forty years, so this is where I call home, too."

"Did you ever know a Gallagher family ower in Rogart?" Hamish asked. "We're trying to track down a Michael Gallagher, known as Mick, who was brought up in the area?"

"I don't recall any Michael Gallagher," Mrs. Roberts said, frowning and shaking her head. "I would know if a boy of that name had attended our school."

"I've no doubt you would," Hamish said, turning to Davey. "Mrs. Roberts knew the name of every child in every year group in our school, and all their parents' names. I wish I had a memory as good as that."

"I haven't been able to help you find this Michael Gallagher, though," said Mrs. Roberts. "Would this have anything to do with the murder up near Scourie by any chance?"

"We can't really say anything," Davey said, knowing full well from the look that Mrs. Roberts gave him that, as far as she was concerned, he'd just said everything, "but how did you know about an incident at Scourie?"

"It was on the TV news earlier," Mrs. Roberts explained. "That lovely reporter who comes from round here, Elspeth Grant, was interviewing a superintendent called Daviot at the crime scene."

"Elspeth's back," Hamish mused. "She's sent up here every time the worst things happen."

"They said a woman's body had been found, but they didn't give her name," said Mrs. Roberts, "and they definitely didn't mention your Mr. Gallagher on the news."

"Our Mr. Gallagher is turning into a bit of a mystery man," Davey said.

"Aye, he is that," Hamish said, heaving his lanky frame out of Mrs. Roberts's sofa. "Now, can you tell me if you've had any other guests staying recently, Mrs. Roberts?"

"None," she said. "Only me and my husband have used the place since we finished the refurbishment."

"Grand," Hamish said. "So I just need to take a wee look in your bathroom. Davey here will keep you entertained wi' facts and statistics and fascinating stories o' police life in Lochdubh!"

Hamish had to duck his head when walking upstairs and had a quick look at the two bedrooms before opening the door to the bathroom. The room was a fresh, modern, white-tiled space with a few charming notes of nautical decoration. There was a walk-in shower behind a glass screen and he dropped to his knees, pulling on a latex glove to unscrew the waste drain cover. There, in the waste trap, he found what he was looking for—a collection of soapy sludge and hair. He scooped it out, dropping it into a clear plastic evidence bag before reassembling the drain cover and heading back downstairs. Davy was in the kitchen with Mrs. Roberts, using a screwdriver on his pocket knife to tighten the screws on the fan window latch.

"That's made it a wee bit more secure, Mrs. Roberts," he said, "but you really need to replace that fastening."

"I will do, Davey," she said. "Thank you for doing that. You're an absolute gem!"

Hamish smiled. The last time he had heard those words, "You're an absolute gem!" had been decades ago when he'd handed in his arithmetic homework with no mistakes. Thanking Mrs. Roberts for the tea, they returned to the Land Rover, where Hamish showed Davey the evidence bag.

"You pulled gunk out of the plughole?" Davey asked.

"Aye, but it's useful gunk," Hamish said. "Mrs. Roberts's hair is short and gray. Her husband hadn't a hair on his head and no one else has used yon shower, so look at this. In among the gunk—a couple o' long dark hairs and a long blonde hair."

"So we now know we're looking for a blonde and a brunette, possibly two brunettes if the girl in the Soutars' shed is separate from the other two," Davey said.

"Aye, but I'm inclined to think there's just the two—two in Mrs. Roberts's house and two in the car. Seems unlikely there would be three o' them wandering Glenmuir. Maybe they just got separated on Wednesday night and the dark-haired one spent the night in the shed," Hamish said, thinking aloud.

"In any case," Davey noted, "we're after the two we know were in Tait's house. We should get a forensics report later today. Maybe we can match a hair if they found anything like that at Tait's house. There might be fingerprints, too, but…"

"The fingerprint team can leave a right mess," Hamish finished Davey's sentence for him, "so let's no' inflict that on Mrs. Roberts unless we really need to. Good thinking, Davey—you're an absolute gem!"

They drove further down the glen to the Loch Muir Inn where there were several cars, vans and trucks in the car park.

"Seems like a popular place," Davey said. "I wouldn't have expected to see so many cars in a place that's so far off the beaten track."

"It's Saturday afternoon," Hamish replied. "There will be football or shinty on a big-screen TV. Still, it's a long way for most to come just for that. You take the lead in here, Davey. I want to have a good look at the place."

"Should I mention Gallagher?"

"Of course. Finding Gallagher and those lassies is still our priority."

Every face in the place turned toward them when they walked in. From a dozen tables scattered across the wooden floor between the ornate, well-lit bar counter and a large picture window that framed a glorious view of the loch, men sitting hunched over their drinks eyed the two police officers with quiet suspicion. By the time Hamish and Davey had strolled up to the bar, most of the customers had turned back to the football match on the giant TV screen near the window and a rumble of conversation resumed.

Davey introduced himself and Hamish to the gray-bearded landlord, who identified himself as Albert. He then politely declined Albert's offer of a drink on the house. He knew there were exceptions to Hamish's Highland hospitality rule and drinking while on duty and in uniform was one of them.

"So what brings the boys in blue—or is it black these days?—to the Loch Muir?" Albert asked.

"We're looking for a couple of young women," Davey explained.

"You're out o' luck there, lads," Albert replied. "I'm afraid this is no' that sort o' place."

There came a few grunts of laughter from the nearest table.

"Funny," Davey said, rewarding Albert with a forced smile. "Two young women, one blonde, one brunette. Have they been in here?"

"I've no' served anyone o' that description in here recently," Albert said. "Now if it was a stubbly, stinky crofter or fisherman you were after," he waved his arm toward his customers, "you could take your pick from this lot."

There were a few more laughs from the drinkers' tables, although no one turned toward the bar, clearly demonstrating they had the ability to eavesdrop without tearing themselves away from the football.

"Actually," Davey said, "there's a fisherman we'd like to talk to as well. Do you know a man named Michael Gallagher?"

"Aye, Mick comes in here from time to time," Albert said. "Can't say as I ken him all that well." He looked to his left, spotted a handy cloth and gave the bar a wipe.

"Do you know anyone who might work with him on his boat?" Davey asked.

"I ken nobody brave enough or bonkers enough to sail on yon clapped out auld hulk," Albert said and there were a few chuckles from the drinkers' tables.

"You know a bit about his boat, then," Davey said.

"No' much, really," Albert replied. "The *Millennium Falcon* is what he named it."

"Like the spaceship in *Star Wars*?" Davey said. "*Millennium Falcon* seems a strange name for a 'clapped out auld hulk.'"

"Aye, but it made the Kessel run in less than twelve parsecs," Albert replied, and two *Star Wars* fans at a nearby table gave him a cheer.

"Quoting Han Solo's not really helping me

find Michael Gallagher, is it, Albert?" Davey said. "Would any of your regulars here know of Gallagher's whereabouts?"

"You can ask them," Albert said, "but they get right grumpy if you interrupt their Saturday afternoon football."

Davey looked to Hamish, who gave an almost imperceptible shake of his head.

"If you hear anything, or if Gallagher shows up here," Davey said, pushing a card across the bar, "let us know."

"Don't hold your breath," Albert said, tucking the card into his pocket.

"And you'd best warn this lot," Davey tilted his head toward the tables of drinkers, "not to be driving up the glen with a drink on them."

"Och, they're all good, law-abiding lads," said Albert, "and there's ay a few designated drivers in among the dedicated drinkers."

Davey urged Albert once again to phone if he heard anything, then he and Hamish made for the door.

"Oh, Constable Forbes..." Albert called from the bar.

"Yes?" Davey turned toward the bar.

"May the police force be with you!" Albert said.

There was another cheer from the *Star Wars* fans and a wave of laughter. Davey grinned at Albert, shaking his head to acknowledge the good-natured teasing before following Hamish out to the car park.

Chapter Five

But there is no kind of dishonesty into which otherwise good people more easily and frequently fall, than that of defrauding government of its revenues, by smuggling when they have an opportunity, or encouraging smugglers by buying their goods.

Benjamin Franklin (1767)

"I'll drive now, if you like," Hamish said and Davey tossed him the car keys. "That was an interesting wee chat you had in there."

"Are you serious?" Davey asked. "I don't think we learned much except the name of Gallagher's boat, and we could have found that out easily enough through the UK Ship Register anyway."

"True, but did you see auld Albert's reaction when you asked about Gallagher?"

"I'm not sure what you're getting at..."

"He was lying, Davey. When he said he didn't know Gallagher all that well, he looked away—broke eye contact wi' you. Every bad liar has a 'tell,' a wee habit that gives them away. Albert's is obviously to look down to his left—a fairly common tell. People who won't look you in the eye don't want you to see what's going on in their heid. He also decided to drag a cloth across the bar, when the bar was perfectly clean and dry. That was a tactic to give him some time to think about how he might answer whatever else you asked about Gallagher. He obviously knows Gallagher, but he told us nothing we couldn't have found out elsewhere."

"I don't suppose we'd have got any more out of his customers," Davey said.

"We'd have got nothing from them. They were all listening, they'd all have had time to think and none of them would have said a thing in front of their drinking pals."

"The bar went a wee bit quiet when we first walked in," Davey said, smiling. "It makes you tend to think people in there had something to hide from us."

"It's ay like that when you visit a pub in uniform," Hamish replied, nodding.

"Sometimes even when you're not in uniform," Davey added, climbing into the Land Rover. "People always seem to know you're a cop, whatever you're wearing. When long hair was fashionable for men, you could easily tell a police officer in a bar by his height and his haircut, but that's really not the case anymore, is it? Short hair's fashionable, and there are plenty of tall blokes. Seems like some people can just see us coming a mile off anyway."

"Easy when we're in uniform, right enough," Hamish agreed, clipping his seatbelt into place but not starting the car. "That's what uniforms are for—so that people who need us can see us straight away. When we're dressed casual, though, those used to dealing wi' the police can spot us plain as day."

"In uniform or not, I can't help feeling suspicious when a bar goes quiet like that. It really does make you think somebody's up to no good."

"And in this case, you'd be right." Hamish started the engine and pulled out of the car park.

"What do you mean?"

"Near everyone in there was drinking whisky." Hamish paused for a moment, letting a car turn into the car park before joining the road. "Maybe no' so unusual in a Highland pub like that, you might think."

"That's pretty much what I'd think, yes," Davey agreed.

"But did you see what whisky they had on offer?"

"Looked like they had the usual stuff," Davey said, concentrating hard on picturing the bar in his mind. "On the optics above the bar they had the Famous Grouse and Dewar's. On the shelf below them I'm pretty sure I saw a bottle of Johnnie Walker and a Lagavulin."

"You did," Hamish agreed. "Mrs. Roberts would give you a gold star for your Look and Learn there—but what was wrong wi' those bottles?"

"Nothing that I noticed," Davey said, feeling confused. "They all looked like the real thing, perfectly clean and fresh."

"Exactly!" Hamish grinned and slapped the steering wheel. "They were all full or near full! The most popular whiskies in Scotland in a bar full o' whisky drinkers and they were practically untouched! Yet to the side was a shelf wi' some grand old whiskies—a twenty-one-year-old Balvenie, a Dalmore o' the same age, a Glenfiddich like the one we liberated from Gallagher's house and a very special Knockando. If you or I were to buy a bottle o' yon Dalmore it would cost more than five hundred pounds and the Knockando would be upward o' seven hundred. Yet those bottles were half empty. Those are what the landlord was serving."

"Really?" Davy's eyebrows shot up. "How many measures can you serve from a bottle?"

"Twenty-eight," Hamish replied, "which makes a single dram…"

"Twenty-five pounds for the Knockando," Davey chimed in, his arithmetic working faster than Hamish's, "before you add on the landlord's overheads and profit."

"There's no way the locals in that place would ever pay that sort o' money for their dram,"

Hamish said, "no matter how beautiful the taste, so that's their guilty secret."

"You think the high-end whiskies are stolen goods?"

"No' stolen exactly," Hamish said, frowning. "Smuggled, more like."

"Scotch whisky being smuggled into Scotland, where it's actually distilled in the first place?" Davey sounded incredulous.

"It's no' such a wild idea when you think that you can buy whisky cheaper abroad, in France or in Spain, than you can in Scotland. Near three-quarters o' the cost o' a bottle here is government tax. Some countries in Europe pay less than a third o' the tax we do."

"So a smuggler could buy whisky from a supplier abroad, then ship it all the way back to Scotland to sell at a profit. The more expensive the whisky, the more profit he stands to make."

"And in a pub like the one we just left, some o' the profit might be sacrificed for a quick sale, maybe even as a reward for helping bring the contraband into the country. Loch Muir's a quiet wee spot for landing contraband."

"The regulars can then sample the delights of the finest single malts for little more than they would pay for their regular dram. It seems almost a shame to deny them that, Hamish, but shouldn't we go back and have a word with Albert? Smuggling is tax fraud, which is a serious crime."

"Let's no' be so hasty," Hamish said slowly, considering their options. "We don't want to let the landlord o' the Loch Muir Inn know that we suspect anything because he'll likely report straight back to the smuggling gang. They'll then go to ground and we might never find out what else they've been up to."

"You think it might be more than a few cases of whisky?"

"Aye, that's more than likely. Once they've set up a supply chain and a route that works for them, they could be bringing in all sorts—maybe even people."

"People? You mean our missing girls?"

"I do. Let's pay Hector another visit and see if he can tell us any more afore we go blundering into the Loch Muir again. If Hector's been offered cheap whisky, he might be able to point us in the direction o' the smugglers without them finding out we're onto them. On our way back to Lochdubh, we can call in on Shona and her father to take her statement."

Andrew MacDougall's house in Braikie was similar to the one his daughter had shared with her husband, although slightly larger. Inside it was clean, tidy and comfortably furnished. Shona was watching TV when Andrew showed Hamish and Davey into the living room but switched it off and walked through to the dining area where they sat together round a table. Hamish then coaxed from her the traumatic story of her husband's latest violent assault.

She shed a few tears while going through precisely what had happened, telling how she had demanded to know where he had been when he turned up at the house in the early hours of the morning, having been gone for a whole day. She struggled a little when describing how his temper had erupted into a flurry of blows that had left her on the floor, bleeding and barely conscious. By the time she felt able to move, he was gone again. Davey diligently wrote down everything she said and Andrew provided the inevitable tea and biscuits. Once Shona had told them everything she could, Davey asked her to sign the statement and he and Hamish prepared to leave.

"That's a fine-looking trophy you have there, Mr. MacDougall," Hamish said, stooping to admire a shining silver cup sitting proudly on the sideboard. Alongside the trophy was a framed photograph of Andrew receiving the award from a woman in a tweed coat, watched by a crowd of men and women gathered at the edge of a field by a drystone wall.

"Aye, that's from the Braikie Drystane Dyke Association," Andrew said. "It's awarded every summer to the champion dyker—the one whose work is judged the best."

"There's a real art to building those walls," Davey said.

"I ken nothing about art," Andrew said, "but it's a skill I was taught as a bairn and one I'm happy to pass on to others. We walk the hills all over Sutherland and repair walls wherever it's needed—wi' the landowner's permission, of course."

"It's a fine thing to be involved wi'," Hamish said, taking a closer look at the photograph, shifting it slightly to catch better light. "The dykes are a real part o' the landscape. Is that your son, James, there among the others in the picture?"

"Aye, we go walking together. He's a skilled dyker himself," said Andrew.

"Does James bide here wi' you?" asked Hamish.

"He does, but he's no' here today," replied Andrew. "He's a heating engineer and he's working on a boiler installation in a hotel on the coast ower near Golspie. He'll be home later."

"Was he working in Golspie afore you all came down to the Piper yesterday?" Hamish asked.

"Aye, he's been on yon job for a while," Andrew said, nodding.

"What's the name o' the hotel?" Hamish asked.

"I mind him telling me," Andrew said, staring

down at the carpet as if concentrating, "but I can't recall the name right now."

"And what about you, Mr. MacDougall?" asked Hamish. "Where were you yesterday afternoon?"

"Shona was happy here on her own," Andrew said, casting his eyes down to the photograph and moving it back to its original position, "so I took myself off for a walk in the hills to get a bit o' fresh air. What's wi' these questions? Why do you need to know where James and I were?"

"We've a possible sighting o' Gallagher yesterday afternoon," Hamish said, offering Andrew a half-truth. "Obviously, finding him is a priority for us after what he did to Shona. Sometimes, when we're looking for someone like Gallagher, it can help to know where people associated wi' him were at the time he was spotted. People sometimes know things or see things that might be important, even if they don't realize it."

"Aye, right," Andrew said, eyeing Hamish suspiciously. "Well, if you get any closer to Gallagher than a 'possible sighting,' you mind and let me know."

Hamish promised, once again, to keep Andrew informed, then he and Davey returned to the Land Rover.

"Was that another of those wee 'tells' I saw in there?" Davey asked, settling himself in the passenger seat.

"If you mean when MacDougall looked down and fiddled wi' the photo," Hamish said, "then, yes, I think it was. He did the same when I asked about the hotel in Golspie. He wasn't telling us the truth."

"He was lying about where he was yesterday?"

"Well, he was only telling us part o' the truth," Hamish said. "He was out in the hills, without doubt, but where in the hills? Yon photograph was taken at Shepherd's house this summer—the old man is there in the picture. The competition they had must have involved rebuilding the wall around his place. That means Andrew and James MacDougall have spent a lot o' time very close to Kathleen Tait's house."

"Do you think they knew her?" Davey asked.

"I think there's every chance they did. They may have seen Gallagher's truck there. James admitted that they knew Gallagher was involved wi' another woman. Maybe the MacDougalls found out it was Kathleen Tait."

"Are we looking at Andrew and James Mac-Dougall as murder suspects? Shepherd didn't mention seeing them at Tait's house yesterday."

"No, but the MacDougalls know Shepherd. They would know that he was watching whoever came and went from Tait's place, and they know the hills. They could have approached from over the hill at the back, where Shepherd wouldn't see them."

"It's possible, Hamish, but why would they kill Tait? It was Gallagher they wanted to get."

"Maybe they tried to force Kathleen Tait to tell them where Gallagher was. Killers or no', they're definitely no' being straight wi' us, Davey. Shona was watching a news bulletin on TV when we arrived. We know Elspeth has been reporting on a murder near Scourie, and she was filming wi' Daviot at the scene—just a stone's throw from where the photo on the sideboard was taken—yet they never mentioned the murder at all."

"Aye, that's weird," Davey agreed. "Anybody

who has two cops in their house would ask about a murder that's happened locally. People like to find out what's going on."

"They do," Hamish said, starting the car, "unless they already know. As far as I'm concerned, we now have five suspects for Kathleen Tait's murder—the two lassies, Gallagher and the two MacDougalls. Start phoning round all the hotels near Golspie, Davey—there aren't that many. Find out if any o' them is having a new boiler fitted. Andrew MacDougall has no real alibi for yesterday afternoon. Let's see if his son's checks out."

"Will do," Davey said, fishing out his phone. "I take it we're off to see Hector MacCrimmon now at the Piper?"

"We are," Hamish confirmed. "He knows far more about Gallagher than he's told us—and if he knows about Gallagher, then maybe he can tell us a bit more about Kathleen Tait, too."

Compared with the Loch Muir Inn, there were relatively few cars parked outside the Piper in

Lochdubh. Hamish parked close to an area of decking outside the pub where customers could sit to enjoy the view out over the loch. There was only one customer on the deck—local fisherman Archie Maclean. Davey slipped his phone into his pocket. None of the hotels he had phoned were having a boiler installed, although he let Hamish know he still had a couple to check out. They both then walked up to greet Archie.

The old fisherman stood, leaning against the wooden rail surrounding the deck, holding a pint of lager in one hand while deftly rolling a cigarette with the other. The only other smokers Hamish had ever seen who could roll a cigarette single-handed were a couple of prisoners he'd regularly escorted from jail to court and back again when he was a young constable. Those old lags had mastered the art of the single-handed roll by necessity, having spent so much time handcuffed to a police officer. He'd never asked Archie how he had learned to do it, preferring to assume it was because he liked to keep one hand on the wheel of his boat.

Archie turned to face them, the floppy sleeve

of his baggy denim jacket sliding up his arm as he settled the cigarette between his lips. He wasn't a large man, but his clothes all looked like they'd been borrowed from a mountainously big brother. His wife was a fanatic about cleanliness, understandably so when her husband regularly came home smelling of beer, cigarettes and fish, and used to boil all the laundry, including Archie's jackets and trousers, in a huge copper. This shrank everything Archie wore, making him look like he was wearing clothes he'd had since he was still at school, until the day he came into some money, buying her a new state-of-the-art washing machine and himself an entire new wardrobe of loose-fitting clothes.

"You're no' out in the boat today, Archie?" Hamish asked.

"Aye, I've been out," Archie grunted. "I set out afore dawn while you were still dead to the world. I landed a fine catch o' sea bass, mackerel and pollock."

"I ken fine your ay up early, Archie," Hamish said, smiling. Archie did not return his smile. He seldom smiled, reluctant to display how few teeth he had. Although happy to have spent his money on clothes, which he needed and wanted, he wasn't prepared to invest in expensive dentistry. He'd enough teeth left to see him to his grave. "Have you no visitors to take out on the water?"

"Tourists are near all gone," Archie said.

"I suppose it's getting to that time of year," Davey said. "School holidays are over and folks with city jobs have to get back to work."

"Maybe," Archie said, "or maybe they've been frightened away."

"Frightened away?" Hamish gave a little laugh. "Whatever could be so frightening about Lochdubh? It's the bonniest place on the planet."

"You say that now," Archie grumbled, lighting his cigarette and drawing in a lungful of smoke, "but there's trouble brewing—you mark my words! I saw them this morning when I was bound for the mouth o' the loch."

"What did you see?" asked Davey.

"Fairy lights on Whuppity Stoorie!" Archie leaked blue smoke from his nose and mouth and pointed west toward the far shore of the loch.

"It's a terrible bad sign. Have you no' seen them yersel', Hamish?"

"I haven't, Archie, but I'll be watching from now on," Hamish assured him.

"Talk to the seer, Hamish," Archie advised, gravely. "He'll ken what's happening wi' Whuppity Stoorie."

"Aye…" Hamish nodded, as though a thought had occurred to him. "Aye, I'll do that, Archie. Now, can you tell me anything about a skipper called Michael Gallagher?"

"Him!" Archie gave a snort of disdain. "He's no skipper. The man's an imposter! I ken nothing about what he does wi' yon fishing boat, but it's no' fishing."

"What do you mean, Archie?" Davey asked.

"He has a bigger boat than mine," Archie replied, "and I've seen it now and again out on the water. He never seems to be headed for any fishing grounds that I ken. I've no idea where he takes yon boat."

"The *Millennium Falcon*," Davey said.

"Is that what he calls it?" Archie snorted. "A right auld rust bucket."

"Och, I don't know about that," Davey said. "She made the Kessel—"

Hamish put a hand on Davey's arm and gave him a look that said, *Forget it*. Archie frowned at them both.

"Do you know where Gallagher berths his boat?" Hamish asked.

"I don't think he uses anywhere on a regular basis," Archie said. "I heard he could be in Ullapool one week, Oban the next and Lochinver the week after. I've never seen him here in Lochdubh, although I've seen the boat at anchor in sheltered coves here and there."

"Maybe he doesn't like paying harbor charges," Davey suggested.

"Aye, maybe," Archie agreed, "but he'll still have to put in to take on fuel when he needs it and pay to land any catch he brings in. Mind you, to catch anything in a boat like that he'd need a crew. At least two if he's fishing, I reckon. He'd get away wi' just one to help him berth the thing in port. Some say one o' his regular crew was a woman."

"What sort o' range would a boat like Gallagher's have, Archie?" asked Hamish.

"Depends how much fuel he has on board," Archie said. "He could easy make it across to Ireland, south into England or even all the way to France."

"Thanks, Archie," Hamish said. "We're just away inside now to have a wee word wi' Hector."

"But you'll visit the seer?" Archie asked. "We don't want any trouble wi' Whuppity Stoorie. The seer will ken what we should do."

"Aye, we'll pay him a visit tomorrow, Archie," Hamish promised, moving to the pub's entrance.

"Oh, and Davey," Archie said, stopping Davey in his tracks, "if I mind right, the *Millennium Falcon* was a smuggler's ship."

Davey looked at Archie, nodded a "thank you" and then followed Hamish into the pub where a few locals were seated at tables nursing last night's hangover with a hair of the dog.

"You know, Archie might have a very good point there, Hamish," Davey said, pausing by an unattended fruit machine that was flashing desperately hungry lights in an attempt to attract players to feed its slot. "If Gallagher hasn't been fishing, what has he been doing with his boat?"

"What indeed?" Hamish said. "And if the landlord o' the Loch Muir knows Gallagher and is selling what might well be smuggled whisky, then we're looking at too much o' a coincidence. We need to check wi' the port authorities up and down the coast to find out if Gallagher has been paying berthing fees or paying to land any kind o' a catch. If he's no' using the boat for fishing, then he's using it for something else and smuggling's starting to look favorite."

"He ran those young women off the road when they were in Tait's car," Davey said. "They're all linked. Could they be his crew?"

"Maybe," Hamish said, "but the two lassies hardly seem like hardened criminals, breaking into Mrs. Roberts's house, leaving it tidy and a bit for the rent besides."

"Yet they were there around the time Tait was murdered," Davey said, "and Shepherd told you one of them was in the house when the shotgun was discharged."

"Aye and they kept themselves hidden when yon cyclist shouted out to them," Hamish said. "They've either got something to hide or they're frightened. The only thing we can be sure about those two is that they're mixed up in a murder, whether they're the killers or not."

"Of course, if Gallagher brought them into the country illegally, they could be hiding from him."

"That's also possible. People smugglers are no' like travel agents. He's no' brought them here for a wee holiday. He's brought them here to make money out o' them, or to pass them on to others who'll make money out o' them."

"Are we talking about prostitution here?" Davey asked.

"Possibly," Hamish said, removing his cap and running his hand through his hair, "but that's a high-risk game wi' some real nasty players. There are easier ways to set them working until such time as whatever debt they owe to the smugglers is paid off."

"So they end up as cheap labor, practically slave labor?"

"Aye, and completely under the control o' Gallagher or whoever he's passed them on to," Hamish said, sighing. "The trouble is, they're no' under control right now and they know all about the smugglers' business. Gallagher can't afford for them to come to us and we know he's a very violent man. For their sake, we need to find those girls afore he does."

They moved off toward the bar, the few customers in the place keenly observing their progress and Hector MacCrimmon, standing behind his bar, watching them approach.

"So what was that other nonsense Archie was on about?" Davey asked. "The silly stuff. Fairy lights? Whuppity-what?"

"Keep your voice down!" Hamish warned him in a low whisper. "You might no' believe in fairies and suchlike, but there's plenty o' folk around here who do. If we're to keep all the locals on our side, I don't want you sounding like you think they're crazy."

"Fine, I'm sorry," Davey said quietly. "So what was bothering Archie so much?"

"Come ower here near the window," Hamish said and they stood together by a large picture window that looked out over the loch to the "Twin Sisters" mountains either side of Hurdie's Glen and the forested slopes that tumbled down to the water way out to the west. The only other people in the bar were well out of earshot, but Hamish kept his voice low nevertheless.

"You see way ower yonder out toward the mouth o' the loch where the trees come right down to the shore?" he said, pointing.

"Aye," Davey said. "Looks like fairly dense forest."

"Well it's no' as dense as it looks," Hamish informed him. "You can't tell from here, but there's a channel a couple o' hundred meters wide that creates an island ower there that's known as Whuppity Stoorie."

Davey folded his arms and gave a slight shake of his head.

"You have to admit," he said, "it's a right silly name."

"Silly to you, no doubt," Hamish replied, "but legend has it that Whuppity Stoorie was a powerful fairy, some say a fairy queen." He paused, frowning, clearly struggling to recall the story of Whuppity Stoorie. "I wish I could mind what they ay used to say about the island, but I haven't heard that auld tale since I was a bairn."

"We're surely not going to waste time on some old folk tale?" Davey said, surprised that Hamish was still taking it so seriously.

"Look, I'm no' for wasting time on anything," Hamish replied, "but we've got some strange goings-on around here right now and talking to the seer's no' such a bad idea. He gets stories from everyone in these parts. Sometimes he can be useful, even if he is an old charlatan."

"You don't believe in fairies, though, do you?"

"Don't be daft, but there's ay more to these fairy stories than you'd think."

"Well, I suppose interviewing the seer will be a new experience," Davey said, grinning.

"Just the men I've been looking for!" Elspeth Grant walked toward them from the main door, smiling broadly.

"Elspeth!" Hamish was always pleased to see his ex-fiancée, even if her trips to Sutherland these days were generally for work rather than pleasure. She gave him a warm hug and awarded Davey the same favor.

If most of the Piper's customers had been distracted by the two police officers before, now that

the cops had been joined by a glamorous celebrity, every face in the pub was turned toward
them. Elspeth was instantly recognizable from
her role on the TV news, although her sleek hair
and designer clothes were a far cry from the curly
mane and charity-shop attire she sported in her
days as a local newspaper reporter, but her captivating, silver-gray eyes still had the power to hold
you in their gaze. Those eyes, more than anything else about her, made it easy to believe her
assertion that the women in her family passed
down a mystical gift of "second sight" from one
generation to the next.

"How did you know we were in here?"
Hamish asked.

"You know we have a special connection,
Hamish Macbeth," she said, teasing him by placing her forefingers on her brow, as though con-
juring up a mental image of him. "All I had to do
was to concentrate hard and...I also saw your
car outside!"

Davey laughed and Hamish smiled, shaking
his head.

"Did I just overhear you talking about going

to see old Angus Macdonald?" Elspeth asked. "It's years since I met the seer. Can I come with you?"

"Well, let's have a chat about that later," Hamish said. "Right now, we need to have a wee word wi' the landlord here."

Hamish and Davey turned to start for the bar again but immediately froze when they saw a young woman standing in the middle of the room. She was holding a huge tray of glasses collected from tables and was staring straight at Hamish and Davey. She had long, dark hair, large dark eyes and high cheekbones that gave her a stunningly beautiful, elfin appearance. She looked slim, athletic and very beautiful, standing perfectly still for just a moment, looking like a startled fawn in the light streaming in from the deck. Hamish broke the spell.

"Could we have a wee word wi' you, miss?" he asked, stepping toward her.

The young woman tensed, looking scared and took a couple of steps backward. Hamish moved forward with Davey at his shoulder and she let out a yell, hurling the tray of glasses at his feet. Hamish slipped on the mess of melting ice, broken glass and beer dregs, falling backward into Davey who stumbled, then tried to move sideways to avoid cannoning into Elspeth. He tripped over a chair leg then fell onto the wooden chair itself so heavily that the legs shattered and he found himself sprawled on the floor.

There was a communal gasp from the Piper's customers but no one made a move to help, and by the time Hamish and Davey were both back on their feet, the young woman had disappeared through the door into the kitchen, screaming "Elena!" at the top of her voice.

"Go out the front, Davey!" Hamish yelled, heading for the kitchen. Davey picked himself up, extricated his foot from part of the chair frame and dashed for the front door.

In the kitchen, a short glance was enough for Hamish to see that the small room was empty. A couple of strides took him to the back door, which was closed and refused to open, clearly having been locked from the outside. He hurried back to the bar and outside to join Davey who was standing in the street, peering right and left but having seen no sign of their quarries.

"Where the hell did they disappear to?" Davey wondered aloud. "Round the back of the houses maybe. If you take the front, streetside, I can—"

"No, Davey," Hamish said. "There's a whole patchwork o' back gardens and allotments behind yon houses—a thousand places to hide—but there's only one way out o' Lochdubh and that's ower the Anstey bridge. Get in the car."

There was no traffic on the road and they raced along the high street until, just beyond the village, Hamish stopped at the bridge, pulling the car across the road to block any vehicles coming in or out of Lochdubh. Leaving the blue lights flashing, they then dismounted and walked back into town, examining any obvious places the fugitives might be hiding. Still they found no trace of the two young women.

"They must still be here somewhere," Hamish said, frustration lending his voice an angry edge. "We'll have to go house-to-house, Davey. I'll see if Jimmy can get us some more uniforms up from Strathbane and—"

His phone rang and he fumbled for it in his

pocket. The voice on the line was as unexpected as it was unwelcome.

"Sergeant Macbeth? It's Helen from Superintendent Daviot's office." The condescending tone made Hamish's temper gauge creep a little further toward the red. He could hear a light clicking sound, which he immediately recognized as Helen tapping a pen against the frame of her glasses, a habit she adopted when she was particularly enjoying deploying the authority of her boss. "The superintendent has ordered you down to Strathbane immediately."

"I'm awful sorry," Hamish said, "but there's a terrible clicking on the line and I can barely hear a word. Maybe you could call back when—"

"Give me that here!" Hamish could hear Jimmy Anderson demanding the phone. "Macbeth, get down here right now!"

"But I'm off duty tonight and—"

"And nothing!" Jimmy snapped. "I don't care what you're doing, I need you here and so does Superintendent Daviot!"

"Aye, okay, Jimmy," Hamish said, resigned to the fact that he couldn't wriggle out of a direct order. "I'm on my way."

*   *   *

Hamish told Davey to do his best knocking on doors to ask about the two girls and walked back to the bridge where a handful of motorists were now queueing either side of the bridge, some looking bemused, others irate at the hold-up. He took a good look at each vehicle on his way past, hoping for some sign of the girls, but saw nothing out of the ordinary. He then climbed into his Land Rover and set off to face Jimmy and Daviot, wondering all the while what could possibly be so important for them to summon him to Strathbane.

It was early evening by the time he pulled into the car park of the large, modern building that was Police Scotland's regional headquarters in Strathbane. The journey had been uneventful, the roads remaining relatively quiet until he had passed through the suburbs into the city-center traffic. Even as he made his way into the building, he could hear the rumble of traffic and feel the grime of the city clinging to him. If there were pleasant areas of Strathbane, Hamish had never encountered them. His experience of the place had always been fraught meetings in this building, seedy drug busts in squalid backstreets or breaking up fights in sleazy pubs or clubs. The only good thing ever to come out of Strathbane, in his opinion, was the road to Lochdubh.

Although it had been months since his previous visit to headquarters, the drab corridors that formed the route to Daviot's office were depressingly familiar. He pushed open the door to the superintendent's outer office and prepared himself for the usual sparring match with Helen.

"Well, Helen," he said, "I'm sure you'll have been missing—"

He stopped in mid-sentence when he stepped into the room to find that Helen was not in her usual place behind her desk. Instead, Jimmy Anderson stood before him, his expression as dark and gray as his suit.

"She'll no' have been missing you at all, laddie," Jimmy said. "She's away home to enjoy her Saturday night, unlike us."

"What's this all about, Jimmy?" Hamish asked.

"You're to be on your best behavior," Jimmy warned him. "Keep a civil tongue in your heid and keep yon temper o' yours under control. We've to go straight in."

"Ah, Sergeant Macbeth, at last," Daviot said as soon as Hamish entered. Superintendent Daviot was not in his usual uniform but was, instead, immaculately attired in a black dinner suit with a black bow tie and a row of miniature medals on his chest. Beside him stood a taller, slimmer man dressed in a uniform Hamish was more accustomed to seeing Daviot wear. On the epaulets of his tunic, however, were a crown and a star, where Daviot only merited a crown. "Chief Superintendent Farnham, allow me to introduce Sergeant Macbeth, our man in Lochdubh."

Farnham gave Hamish a curt nod. He was younger than Daviot and had dark eyes that seemed to soak up his surroundings, giving the impression of a man who missed nothing. Hamish nodded an acknowledgment.

"And, of course, Sergeant Macbeth," Daviot said with hesitant cough, "you…um…already know DCI Blair."

Hamish shot a look to his left where stood the portly, disheveled figure of Blair, a man with whom Hamish had crossed swords many times in the past. His blue suit had accordion creases at the crooks of the arms and, baggy though it was, the jacket's three sad buttons knew they'd never meet their buttonholes again. Blair was a despicable, dishonest disgrace of a police officer whom Daviot had succeeded in banishing to Glasgow, although he'd since spun back to Strathbane more often than a homesick boomerang.

For years, Blair had dominated Daviot, despite Daviot being a more senior officer, using compromising photographs of Daviot's wife, taken when she had been drugged. Blair had elicited favors, forced the turning of a blind eye to his underhanded endeavors and demanded leniency for his misdeeds. Eventually, Daviot had appealed to Hamish for help, relying on the Highlander to recover the pictures and save his wife's reputation, whereupon Blair was sent packing. So what was he doing back this time? Who was Farnham and what were they up to?

"You'd no' make much o' a poker player,

Macbeth," Blair said, a smarmy smile forcing his jowly cheeks apart. "A blind haggis could tell what you're thinking. You're wondering what we're all doing here, are you no'? Well, you're about to find out."

Chapter Six

It is very unfair to judge any body's conduct, without an intimate knowledge of their situation.
Jane Austen, *Emma* (1815)

Kira and Elena huddled together in the darkness, sharing the last piece of shortbread they had stolen from the window ledge in Lochdubh. Elena stared at her friend and, even though she could barely make out her features, she knew Kira was looking every bit as lost and frightened as she was. They had started their journey together full of hope, yet now it seemed like the whole world had turned against them. Now their future seemed as utterly black and miserable as the night sky above them.

"This is all," Kira said, nibbling on the short-bread. "After this we have no more food."

"We will find food from somewhere," Elena assured her.

"But how?" Kira asked, fighting back a sob. "We have no money! We have no passports. If only I had..."

"Don't blame yourself," Elena hugged Kira closer. Usually, Kira was the practical one but after all that had happened, Elena knew she now had to play her part, and right then that meant she had to be strong and comfort her friend. "There was nothing more you could have done. If you had not acted, we might both now be dead."

"I'm so sorry, Elena," Kira said, finally shedding a tear, "but when gun went off, there was so much mess. Insides of chair were everywhere, furniture was knocked over and then she was lying on floor. Maybe she was lying on passports and money. I should have moved her..."

"Hush now—don't cry," Elena said. "There was no time. You did well and we are free. Together we will find a way out of this place."

"How can we do that without passports or

money?" Kira sighed. "Passports will now be with police or back with that man they call Mick."

"We will manage," Elena assured her. "We always manage together."

"But now we are hunted," Kira whimpered, "by that man and by police. What will happen to us if we are caught by police? In this country, do they execute people for murder?"

Straightening his dinner jacket and adjusting the small display of miniature medals above the breast pocket, Superintendent Daviot then glanced at his watch and looked toward Chief Superintendent Farnham.

"You are, naturally, welcome to use my office for as long as you need, sir," Daviot said, and Hamish was convinced by the man's body posture that he was somehow resisting the urge to bow, "but, as you know, I have an important engagement at the Town Hall and I'm running a little late."

"Yes, of course, you must go, Peter," Farnham said, dismissing Daviot with another of the nods that seemed to be his preferred mode of communication. Daviot hurried out the office door and Blair stepped a little closer to Farnham with a cocky swagger. Clearly, he wanted to confirm where his loyalties lay and demonstrate to Jimmy and Hamish that he and the chief superintendent were a team.

"You've had a bit o' excitement up there in your wee backwater, Macbeth," Blair said, attempting a smile but achieving only a lopsided sneer. "No' your usual missing cats and stolen bicycles."

Farnham turned his head slowly and stared coldly at Blair, his features impassive, his eyes unblinking. Blair immediately clammed up and stepped backward, seeming to shrink a little.

"I'll keep this brief, Sergeant," Farnham said, turning to face Hamish again. "You are aware of a connection between the murdered woman, Kathleen Tait, and Michael Gallagher."

"Aye, I am," Hamish agreed.

Farnham paused, giving Hamish the same cold stare to which he had treated Blair, leaving Hamish in no doubt that his response had been lacking in etiquette.

"I am, *sir*," Hamish said, deciding that a staring game and waiting contest would only drag out the time he had to spend in Strathbane even further.

"Michael Gallagher is now a suspect in the murder of Kathleen Tait," Farnham said, stating the fact concisely. "We have an interest in Gallagher beyond the murder investigation."

"What interest would that be, sir?" Hamish asked, soliciting a tut from Jimmy for his interruption.

"That's none of your concern, Sergeant," Farnham said. "Suffice to say that we want him found as quickly as possible. I will be coordinating efforts outside of your patch. DCI Anderson will remain in charge of the overall murder investigation and you are to concentrate on locating Gallagher."

"How do we know he's still on my patch, sir?" Hamish asked.

"We don't," Farnham replied, "but you are to leave no stone unturned—do you understand? All of your efforts are now to be directed toward finding Gallagher. To that end, DCI Blair will be joining you in Lochdubh tomorrow afternoon."

"What? Why him?" Hamish objected, a note of clear indignation in his voice.

"Because DCI Blair knows Gallagher of old," Farnham said, ignoring Hamish's outburst in an effort to bring the meeting to a close as swiftly as possible. "He can identify Gallagher and any of his former associates should they also come looking for him."

"Former associates?" Hamish muttered, looking from Farnham to Blair. Blair smirked, obviously enjoying the big Highlander's discomfort.

"You know your patch," Farnham went on, "he knows the faces. He will join you in Lochdubh tomorrow, Sergeant, and you'll work as a team. Now, I'd like to talk to DCI Blair, so if you've no further questions, you may go, gentlemen."

"Hold on a wee minute—" Hamish began, but Jimmy clamped a hand on his arm.

"I need a word, Sergeant," he said, encouraging Hamish toward the door.

"And Macbeth," Farnham called, halting Hamish and Jimmy in their tracks. Hamish looked round to face the senior officer's cold, hard glare and what sounded like a threat. "Don't let me down, Sergeant."

Hamish followed Jimmy to the empty outer office and then along the corridor, turning left into an open area where there were rows of gray desks on which sat gray computer screens and in front of which sat gray, weary detectives working the nightshift. The majority of the desks were empty and those officers they did walk past neither acknowledged their presence nor even looked up from their work. Jimmy's office was behind a glass partition at the far end of the room. He sank into the chair behind his desk and motioned Hamish to close the door.

"What's going on, Jimmy?" Hamish asked. "Why am I being landed wi' yon scunner Blair? He's bound to be more of a hindrance than a help and—"

"Listen, laddie," Jimmy interrupted, "we both need to keep our heids here. I'm no' being told any more than you've just been told, but orders have come down from on high. Daviot's running scared and wants nothing to do wi' this thing, otherwise he'd never agree to Blair being involved. He doesn't want any bad marks on his record so close to him picking up his pension, so I think he's relieved to be handing it all over to Farnham, but I hear this thing goes way up the chain o' command—way beyond Daviot or Farnham."

"What 'thing'?" Hamish said, a scowl of frustration on his face. "How do they expect us to do our jobs when we're no' being told everything?"

"Well, in all my years, I've only seen this happen once afore," Jimmy said. "You ken we've no' released the name o' the murder victim yet."

"Aye," said Hamish. "We don't do that until the relatives have been informed."

"That's just the thing, Hamish—we can't find any relatives," Jimmy said, lowering his voice even though there was no one to hear them. "Kathleen Tait was registered to vote, registered to pay taxes to the local council, owned a flat in Strathbane and that house out near Scourie, but we can't find any trace o' her parents nor any brothers, sisters or any other kin at all. She never made friends wi' any o' her neighbors and, as far as we can tell, she never had any job, although she wasn't claiming social security benefits."

"Sounds almost like she didn't exist," Hamish said. "We had a bit o' the same wi' Gallagher—no relatives or friends at his wedding and no one who minds him growing up in Rogart."

"That's to be expected," Jimmy said, leaning back in his chair. "They're hollow people, Hamish—fake names, fake identities created for them by the powers that be. They've been involved in some nasty business down south and been given a fresh start up here in return for giving evidence against what Farnham called their 'former associates.'"

"Is that so?" Hamish frowned, thinking it through. "That would explain why Blair's involved. He's lived his whole life wi' one foot in the gutter. He knows more scumbags than my cousins have got cousins. We don't want any o' Blair's gangster pals involved. Things will get messy."

"That's another reason for no' releasing Tait's name," Jimmy said.

"Aye, but an anonymous murder victim becomes a story in itself for the media," Hamish said, "and people who lived near Tait's house up by Scourie will know what's happened already after the police were at the house. It's only a matter o' time afore the name leaks out. Then the media will somehow find a picture o' Tait to put on TV. Those she was sent up here to hide from will recognize her and come looking for Gallagher."

"Blair should be able to warn us o' that, but you have to keep an eye on him, Hamish," Jimmy said, knowing that the two men had been at each other's throats in the past. "He's a right evil little swine and no' to be trusted. Best thing we can do now is exactly what Farnham says—find Gallagher fast. Any help you need, come to me. Now, what's been happening in Lochdubh?"

"Well, it makes sense that Gallagher and Tait had a criminal past, because it looks like they've been up to no good again..."

Hamish updated Jimmy on the missing girls, the suspected smuggling operation and the list of murder suspects. He omitted to mention that he and Davey had let the girls slip through their fingers in the Piper, and then a thought suddenly occurred to him.

"Jimmy, the new landlord o' the Piper is Hector MacCrimmon," he said, slapping a hand to his forehead. "He says he's an auld friend o' Gallagher's. If he knows him from his previous life, then at least one o' the 'former associates' might already be in Lochdubh!"

By the time Hamish was driving down from the high road onto the bridge outside Lochdubh, his tired eyes welcomed the sight of the streetlights. Out on the road from Strathbane, his car headlight beams had been the only illumination and, even though he knew the route well, concentrating on the road with thoughts of Gallagher and Blair filling his head had worn him down. He suddenly realized he was also feeling hungry and that he hadn't eaten since breakfast. It was now well past supper time, and a gentle alarm bell rang in his head, although he couldn't quite work out why. When he came within sight of his police station, the alarm bell turned to a klaxon and he winced. Parked next to Davey's car in the street by his front gate was Claire's car.

It was Saturday night—they were supposed to have gone out to dinner! This was going to be a wee bit awkward...

He parked the car and walked down the side path toward the back door, then paused. He could hear laughter and the clinking of glasses coming from his kitchen. The door was open and he stopped short of the light cascading out onto the path, standing in the shadows to listen.

"...so then Hamish slipped on all the ice and broken glass and knocked Davey backward into me, but he sidestepped me and took out a chair—smashed it to bits!"

There were peels of laughter. Hamish recognized Elspeth's voice accompanied by Claire and Davey's laughter.

"Davey Forbes, the great rugby player," Claire said, sucking in huge breaths, "and Hamish Macbeth, the champion hill runner, couldn't catch two wee lassies!"

Hamish prided himself on having a fine sense of humor and, funny though the story was, it didn't really merit quite the level of hilarity that was being generated. When he stepped into the light, he could see that the fourth player in Elspeth, Claire and Davey's pantomime was a bottle of Glenmorangie. Whisky is guaranteed to turn even a mildly amusing story into the most hysterical tale you've ever heard.

"Well, well, talk o' the devil," Claire said, and the kitchen fell silent. "Were we no' supposed to be out this evening planning a wee break somewhere warm and sunny?"

"Aye, well…look, I'm really sorry, Claire, but…" Hamish began, but Claire was on her feet standing right in front of him in an instant, looking seriously vexed.

"It's a good job you've got Davey looking after you now," she said. "He phoned to tell me you were in Strathbane."

"I'll make it up to you, Claire, honestly," Hamish promised.

"Too right you will," Claire told him, then reached up to wrap her arms round his neck, drew his head toward her and kissed him. "Now come in and sit down, you big galoot. I made a fish pie to bring wi' me and there's plenty left for you."

He caught the twinkle of mischief in her eyes

but saw no anger there, realizing she'd been teasing him and chiding himself for falling for it. Falling for it, or falling even further for her? Definitely a bit of both. Then the kitchen was filled with chat and laughter once again, Claire serving him a plateful of food and Davey filling a glass for him. Lugs and Sonsie then erupted into the room to join the party, having returned from a late prowl along the beach, Lugs demanding attention from everyone while Sonsie pestered only Hamish.

"Relax, Hamish," Elspeth said softly, fixing him with her misty gray eyes, her lips barely moving but her words seeming to cut through the din perfectly clearly so that only he could hear. "You need this time. This is the calm before the storm."

The following morning Davey bounced downstairs, his hair still wet from his shower, to find Hamish and Claire washing dishes at the kitchen sink.

"Morning, Davey," Claire greeted him, looking

over her shoulder. "There's some breakfast for you keeping warm under the grill. Feeling bright and breezy after last night, are we?"

"Aye, I'm fine," Davey replied. "We didn't have too much to drink and I had some fresh air walking Elspeth back to the Tommel Castle."

"She's a lucky lass having the company pay for her to stay there," Claire said, nudging Hamish. "I'd like to stay in a nice hotel somewhere, too!"

"Och, you know I'll sort something out as soon as this murder business—" Hamish began, but Claire cut him off with a hug.

"We'll sort something out together," she said, smiling. "You've been working hard for months and you deserve a break, especially now you've got Davey here to hold the fort!"

"Aye, once we get this business with those girls and Gallagher sorted out, you can leave me in charge!" Davey said, grinning and retrieving a plate from the grill and sniffing the bacon and eggs. "Thanks for this, Claire, I'm fair starving!"

Claire left for work and Hamish sat at the table with Davey, filling him in on what had happened in Strathbane.

"DCI Blair back here?" Knowing the background between the two men, Davey was surprised.

"Aye," Hamish sighed, running a hand through his hair, "the man's more difficult to shake off than shite on your shoe, but we're stuck wi' him. I want to visit auld Angus and Hector MacCrimmon afore Blair gets here, so let's get moving."

"Umm...Hamish," Davey said, rising slowly from his seat, "I seem to recall that some kind of gift or offering's required when visiting the seer."

"Aye, you're right, Davey," Hamish agreed. "We'll have to pop down to the Patels' shop for a Dundee cake and...Crivens! It's Sunday! The Patels don't open until the afternoon!"

"How about this?" Davey reached into a kitchen cupboard and retrieved the bottle of whisky from Gallagher's house.

"No' the Glenfiddich..." Hamish groaned. "All right, let's take it, but we better get some rare words o' wisdom out o' the auld bugger for that!"

Having agreed that Elspeth, who wanted to

seek out some "local color" for her next TV news report on the murder, could come with them on their visit to the seer, Hamish and Davey picked her up from the hotel. They parked the Land Rover at the edge of a meadow on the outskirts of the village, then walked along a path that wound its way toward a slope, rising steeply to where Angus Macdonald's cottage sat on a level, grassy area. Hamish had always maintained that, from this vantage point, Angus could use binoculars to spy on the good people of Lochdubh, learning small secrets that he could later "reveal" in one of his fortune-telling sessions. He had felt tempted on several occasions to arrest the old man for fraud, but the seer's network of clients and contacts meant that he could sometimes supply useful tidbits of information. There would also be a massive outcry from the locals should he lock up someone providing them with what many saw as an essential service.

The seer's ancient cottage had thick stone walls and small windows to keep the heat in and the cold out. Wisps of smoke rising from the chimney showed that peat was burning in his fireplace. Hamish was about to rap his knuckles on the front door when he realized that the peeling paint he expected to see had been renewed in a lustrous, dark red and there was a large, polished brass knocker in the shape of a burning sun. Before he could try out the knocker, the door swung open and the seer stood on the threshold.

Angus Macdonald somehow managed to appear more like a caricature of a mystic every time Hamish saw him. His head, previously adorned with white hair that reached down beyond his shoulders, was now completely bald and decorated with a black velvet skullcap embroidered with peculiar gold symbols. His white beard was as long and straggly as ever, sitting over a faded gray kaftan that reached the floor.

"I see you've a new front door, Angus," Hamish said, brightly.

"A new coat does not make a new man," Macdonald said, sagely, staring in Hamish's direction with a practiced, glassy myopia. "Welcome Macbeth ... and friends. Come ben."

They followed Angus into the one main room

of the cottage that was his kitchen, living area and consulting room. The space was dark, lit only by the fire in the hearth, daylight filtering through the grubby windows and candles in glass jars, although, to the best of Mrs. Roberts's Look and Learn students, the candles' all-too-regular flickering betrayed them as battery powered.

The seer offered Elspeth one of the well-worn leather armchairs by the fire and she sniffed the air as she sat, enjoying the sweet scent of burning peat. Davey brought two high-backed Orkney chairs from across the room and they gathered round the fire.

"We brought this gift for you," Hamish said, reluctantly producing the whisky from where he had it clasped protectively in his arms.

"A gift indeed," Macdonald remarked, his white eyebrows shooting up toward the velvet cap and his eyes suddenly sharply focused. "A sight better than the usual fruitcake." He rose from his seat, taking the bottle to a cupboard, which he unlocked using a key on a string around his neck. Once the Glenfiddich was safely locked away, the key disappeared back behind his beard and he resumed his seat.

"Ask what you will," Macdonald said sagely, "and I will answer as I can."

"We need to find a man called Michael Gallagher," Hamish said. "Do you know where he is?"

"When a man prefers not to be found," Macdonald said, gazing into the fire, "you must look where he prefers to be. You will find him on the water. More I cannot say."

"We're also looking for two young women," Davey said. "Can you tell us anything about them?"

"They're too quick for two Highland plods, is what I heard," Macdonald chuckled. Hamish rolled his eyes and Elspeth stifled a giggle. "They have come far and yet have far to go," Macdonald went on. "They have the look of those from another land, perhaps another realm."

Hamish sighed. As usual, Angus was telling them pretty much what they already knew, wrapped up in the language of fairy stories. That thought reminded him of Archie.

"Archie Maclean told us he'd seen lights on

Whuppity Stoorie," Hamish said. "Anything you can tell us there?"

"Whuppity Stoorie must not be disturbed!" Angus looked at Hamish, eyes wide with genuine horror. "Her island must not be violated!"

"Why is that, Mr. Macdonald?" Davey asked. "Where does the name Whuppity Stoorie come from?"

"Whuppity Stoorie was a fairy queen," Macdonald said, closing his eyes and leaning back in his chair. "They say she mastered the most powerful magic ever known and had lived for ower a thousand years, although she still had the look and form o' a beautiful young woman. Whuppity was rich and wise and had everything anyone might desire except for one thing. Through all her long years she had never been in love, nor found anyone who truly loved her and, despite the accumulated wisdom of her years, she had no idea how to find love."

"Is this going to take much longer?" Hamish said, looking at his watch. Davey and Elspeth hushed him.

"Finally, despairing of ever finding love and

happiness, Whuppity decided to cross into the realm of men..." Macdonald stared at Hamish, "...and women..." he added, looking at Elspeth, "...and the LGBTQIA plus community," he finished, his eyes settling on Davey.

"Angus, I don't think that Davey is—" Hamish started to say, but the old man held up a hand to silence him, staring at Davey.

"Maybe no'," he said. "Constable Forbes is everything he appears to be, yet he holds a secret close to his heart..."

Davey lowered his head and glowered at the old man.

"It's no' a secret he holds wi' pride, but a secret o' which he is ashamed," Macdonald said. "It's a personal shame...a family shame...yet beneath the fallen, crumpled leaves o' shame, a bloom o' love strives to open into the light."

"Angus," Elspeth said gently, trying to save Davey any further embarrassment, "can you get back to Whuppity?"

"Aye, aye..." the old man said, leaning back in his chair again. "Whuppity wandered the hills around Lochdubh in the sunshine until she heard the sound o' singing and followed the sound until she saw a young farmer, Gregor, harvesting barley in his field. She watched him work and listened to him singing until he became aware o' her presence. He looked toward her, their eyes met and in that instant Whuppity and Gregor fell deeply in love.

"Whuppity sat talking wi' Gregor for hours on end. Ower the coming days, she helped him wi' his work, cooked and ate wi' him, but returned to her own realm every night. Then, at the end o' another day, she decided she wanted to stay and asked to share his bed. She knew that if she lay wi' a mortal man she could never return to the fairy realm and would be doomed to live a mortal life. She did so anyway, and they spent the rest o' their living days together.

"Many years passed and when their eyes had dimmed and their bodies had grown frail, Gregor laid down on the hillside one day, knowing that he would never rise again. He asked one last question o' Whuppity: 'Why did you choose to stay wi' me all these years?'

" 'You know well, my love,' she said. 'I lived a

thousand years and might have lived a thousand more but I would trade them all again for one night in your arms. Now we shall be together for all eternity.'

"She lay down at his side and when his eyes closed for the last time, she drew her cloak over him. The hillside broke away from the mainland and drifted out into the loch to form an island. There they have rested together ever since."

"It's a lovely story," Elspeth said, wiping what might have been a tear from the corner of her eye, "but why were you so concerned about the island being disturbed?"

"Because if any should desecrate the last resting place o' Whuppity Stoorie," Macdonald said, waving a warning finger, "she'll send a plague that will wipe out every living person in the land!"

Hamish, Davey and Elspeth walked back down the hill to the Land Rover in silence. Davey avoided any eye contact, clearly praying that neither Hamish nor Elspeth should ask him about any shameful secret. Once they were all back in the car, Hamish finally turned to Davey.

"Well, Davey, I think auld Angus has given us another wee problem," he said.

"What do you mean?" Davey asked nervously.

"We need to get a boat and check out Whuppity Stoorie."

"Really?" Davey said, sounding both incredulous and very relieved. "Are you really worried about a fairy queen unleashing a plague on us?"

"Of course not," Hamish said, starting the car, "but Angus will now tell that story to anybody as cares to listen. Some people will take it very seriously and the island's no' a safe place. The currents around it are tricky and there's no proper landing stage for a boat. I don't want anybody taking risks visiting the island trying to save the world, so we need to find out what Archie's mysterious lights are all about."

"There's always a nugget of truth in all these old stories, you know," Elspeth said from the back seat.

"Aye, right," Hamish said, eyeing her in the rear-view mirror. "Nuggets to that."

*   *   *

When they dropped Elspeth back at the hotel, Priscilla appeared on the front steps, almost as if she had been waiting for them. Dressed casually in a powder-blue cashmere sweater and precisely faded, tight jeans, she strolled over to the car, exchanging a pleasant greeting with Elspeth before concentrating her attention on the passenger window, and Davey.

"I know you must be terribly busy," she said, looking up at him with big, blue eyes, "but it would be nice to see you here at the hotel, maybe for a drink sometime."

"Aye, well that would be nice," Davey said, talking through the open window, the car door remaining firmly closed. "We'll maybe do that when, as you say, we're a wee bit less busy."

Hamish noticed none of the preening and posing he had seen when Davey and Priscilla had previously met. It was as though a change had come over the young man. He was polite, yet reluctant to fully engage in conversation with her. The colonel then appeared, calling to

Priscilla that he needed to talk to her about the new menus, and she gave Davey a generous parting smile.

"I suppose we're all busy," she said, "but let's make some time soon."

"Aye, we'll do that," Davey said, a note of relief in his voice. "Now we have to be off, don't we, Hamish?"

They said their goodbyes and Hamish set off down the driveway toward the main road.

"You don't seem quite so keen to see Priscilla right now," he said to Davey. "Have you no' got the hots for her anymore?"

"No...well, aye...but..." Davey shifted in his seat. "Maybe it was something auld Angus said, or maybe...let's just leave it, Hamish. I'm feeling a wee bit out of sorts right now."

"No worries," Hamish said with a shrug, "let's concentrate on Hector MacCrimmon."

It took just a few minutes to reach the Piper, where Hector was standing behind the bar.

"Don't take this the wrong way, lads," he said, "but the pair o' you marching in here in uniform every day might no' be good for business. People are going to start wondering why the police are ay in my pub."

"We'll try no' to make a habit o' it, Hector," Hamish said, "but I need to talk to you about those two lassies who were in here yesterday."

"I told Constable Forbes everything already," Hector said.

"So now tell me," Hamish replied. "Who are they?"

"They said they were hitch-hiking across the country," Hector said, leaning on the bar and fixing Hamish with a stare. "I never seen them afore yesterday. They said they were broke and asked if they could do a bit o' work for a square meal."

"That's no' the usual way landlords take on staff," Hamish pointed out.

"Maybe no'," Hector agreed, "but they were good-looking lassies and it never hurts to have the likes o' them about the place. Customers like pretty staff."

"Did you talk to them much?" Hamish asked.

"No' really," Hector answered. "Their English wasn't that great."

"What sort of accent did they have?" asked Hamish.

"Sort o' Eastern European or maybe Russian," Hector said. "The accent kind o' suited their look."

"So they weren't sent here to work for you?" asked Davey.

"Who on earth would send me two good-looking lassies to work here?" Hector said, raising his eyebrows. "This is a wee village pub, no' the Moulin Rouge!"

"When did you first meet Michael Gallagher?" Hamish asked.

"A few years back," Hector replied, the question bringing a look of suspicion to his eyes. "He used to buy and sell things, and I knew people who sold and bought things, so our paths crossed a few times."

"Did he always go by the name Michael Gallagher?" Davey asked.

"No idea," Hector said. "I only ever knew him as Mick."

"You gave us his name as Michael Gallagher when you pointed out his wife and her family to us on Friday evening," Hamish said.

"Aye, but I never knew him as that until I met him up here," Hector asserted. "He showed up one day just after I bought the place. I hadn't even moved in. He came to say hello when I was dealing wi' some workmen."

"Just hello?" Hamish asked. "Maybe it was more than that. Maybe he offered you some cheap whisky."

"Look," Hector said, letting out a long sigh. "I'm no' saying whether he did or he didn't, but I wouldn't take a dodgy deal on high-end whisky. If I'm to make a go o' running this place, I need to keep everything absolutely above board. You're welcome to take a look in the stock room and anywhere else you like, Sergeant Macbeth, but you'll no' find anything that I can't account for down to the last penny."

"You know what, Hector?" Hamish said, staring the old fighter straight in the eye. "I believe you. So what did he tell you about his wife and her family?"

"He was feared o' them," Hector said. "Told me they were a bad bunch. Said the three o' them drank together whenever he was away working and the father and brother would fight—even fought wi' Shona and sometimes left her in a right state. He tried to get her to go away wi' him to live somewhere else, but she wouldn't leave them. They blamed him whenever she got hurt and he came to blows wi' the father and brother. He threatened to report them but she wouldn't let him do that. He said Shona warned him her father and brother were planning to kill him, Sergeant Macbeth, and I've no' seen him since."

"Okay, Hector," Hamish said, "but if Gallagher ever gets in touch wi' you again, I want to know about it."

"Aye, aye, of course," Hector assured him. "Whatever that lot have been up to, I don't want…" Hector's face then darkened as he looked over Hamish's shoulder. "Bloody hell," he cursed, "what's that scunner doing here?"

Hamish turned to see DCI Blair enter the bar, wearing the same forlorn blue suit he'd worn in Daviot's office.

"I thought you must be skiving off in here when I saw yon car outside," Blair barked, advancing to confront Hamish. The Land Rover, with its distinctive, blue-and-yellow "Battenberg" livery, was designed to have high visibility, but this was the first time Hamish had seen cause to regret it being so easy to spot. "How did you come by a new car like that? No other police in our region have one o' those."

"Daviot swung it," Hamish said. "Somebody he knows at his golf club has a dealership and in return for a bit o' publicity and a few photos they could use in advertising, they offered a good deal on the car."

"Och, I see…" Blair smirked. "The auld pals' act, is it? You scratch my back and I'll… Well, I'll be buggered—if it's no' Hector MacCrimmon!"

"You're safe enough then, Mr. Blair," Hector said, "because it is Hector MacCrimmon."

"You're a bit out o' your comfort zone away up here in the back o' beyond, are you no', Hector?" Blair said, his face switching from surprise back into sneer mode.

"I moved up here as a kind o' retirement," Hector explained. "If I can make it work, this place will give me a decent living."

"Well, it makes a change from getting your

brains bashed out in a boxing ring or working as a nightclub bouncer," Blair said. "I might even wander in for a drink later. We can talk over auld times, eh?"

Hector looked distinctly unenthusiastic about renewing any acquaintance with Blair and said nothing. Blair then turned to Hamish.

"I'm off to check in at the Tommel Castle," he said. "Meet me in here in an hour. You can update me then on any progress you and the boy wonder have made, although I doubt that'll take long."

"I'd rather do that at the station," Hamish said.

"Just do as you're told, Macbeth!" Blair snapped, then turned on his heel and left.

Hamish gritted his teeth, staring out the pub door at the portly figure struggling into a nondescript saloon car in the car park.

"He hasn't changed," Davey said, bleakly.

"The likes o' Blair never do," said Hamish, slowly.

His phone then rang and he plucked it from his pocket, noting from the screen that the caller was Mrs. Patel.

"Hamish! We've been robbed!" Mrs. Patel sounded distraught. "They came in, took a load o' stuff and ran off! I couldn't get hold o' them and—"

"Calm yourself, Mrs. Patel," Hamish said gently. "We're no' far away. We'll be right there."

Hamish and Davey jumped into the Land Rover and sped down the shore road to where the Patels' general-store-cum-post office, now proudly boasting a new shop sign that proclaimed it to be the "Lochdubh Mini-market," nestled close to the trees leading up to the bridge. Mrs. Patel stood at the shop's front door, wringing her hands with worry.

"Thank goodness you're here, Hamish!" she said, her voice charged with anguish. "I couldn't catch them—they were too quick for me."

"Are you all right, Mrs. Patel?" Hamish asked. "Did they hurt you at all?"

"No, they just grabbed some stuff and ran off," she replied.

"Did you get a good look at them, Mrs. Patel?" Davey asked. "What did they look like?"

"It was two young women," Mrs. Patel

explained. "One wi' blonde hair, one wi' dark hair. Nice-looking lassies and very polite when they came in—said 'Good morning.' I pointed out it was now the afternoon and they took that as a wee joke. They walked round the shelves like they were shopping, and then ran out the door. I screamed at them to stop, but they ignored me. Mr. Patel's gone out looking for them in his van."

"Call him and tell him to come home, Mrs. Patel," Hamish said. "We'll look for your shop-lifters. Sounds like we've already had dealings wi' them. What did they take?"

"Basic stuff—bread, milk, cold meat, chocolate—nothing very dear."

"Did you see which way they went?" Davey asked.

"They were gone by the time I got out from behind the counter," Mrs. Patel said, shaking her head, "but I did notice one thing about them when they were running out the door. They both looked like they'd wet their pants."

"Is that right?" Hamish said. "I know you yelled at them, Mrs. Patel, but I don't think you're really that scary..."

"I know, and it looked right strange," Mrs. Patel explained. "They were both wearing jeans and they both had big wet patches on...you know...their backsides. And I'm sure I heard one o' them shout 'sorry' on their way out."

"Let's take a look around, Davey," Hamish said. "You go back toward the pub and I'll go out to the bridge."

An hour later, they met back at the shop, having found no sign of the two young women anywhere.

"Have you not found them?" Mr. Patel said, marching out of his shop. "This is a disgrace! We run a vital business in this community! We should not be at the mercy of robbers and thieves."

"I couldn't agree more, Mr. Patel," Hamish said. "I don't want thieves running around Lochdubh any more than you do, believe me."

"It's like they just vanished into thin air," Davey said, "and they're the most unlikely criminals—breaking in and leaving rent money, then apologizing for shoplifting."

"They're no' really criminals at all, Davey,"

Hamish said, scratching his chin and thinking hard. "I think they're just two frightened lassies on the run. Still…no' frightened enough to wet…wait a wee minute. Davey, when the outward-bound center was broken into, what was stolen?"

"They were still checking the stock in their shop, but they gave me a preliminary list," Davey said, fumbling for his notebook and flicking through the pages. "Umm…a couple of sleeping bags, a pop-up two-person tent and a kayak."

"A kayak…" Hamish said, opening the car door and grabbing a pair of binoculars. He stood on the door sill and used the binoculars to look out across the loch. "Would that have been a blue and green kayak, Davey?"

"It was," Davey confirmed.

"There's your two shoplifters, Mr. Patel," Hamish said, pointing into the distance near the far shore of the loch. "That's how they got wet bums—sitting in a kayak."

"And that's how they gave us the slip before," Davey said, shielding his eyes to peer at the two figures in the small boat, only just managing to pick them out against the trees. "They didn't disappear into thin air—they took to the water."

"And look where they're heading," Hamish said, handing the binoculars to Davey. "I'm guessing the outward-bound center will find torches or lanterns have also gone missing from their shop. Our two fugitives are behind Archie's mysterious lights on Whuppity Stoorie!"

Chapter Seven

There are moments in every man's life when he feels he's invincible.
John Buchan, *The Thirty-Nine Steps* (1915)

Hamish threw the keys to Davey and hurried round the car to the passenger seat, pulling out his phone and tapping a speed-dial number.

"Where to?" Davey asked, starting the engine.

"Down to the harbor, Davey, quick as you like," Hamish said, then concentrated on his phone as the call went through. "Archie, I need to borrow your boat. No, no' the fishing boat, just your wee dinghy. Aye, I know the boats are how you make a living, but we need to get ower to Whuppity Stoorie to sort out those lights. No, we'll no' disturb anything—we'll put a stop to any disturbances. Thanks, Archie. We'll be there in a couple o' minutes."

They raced down the shore road toward Lochdubh's small harbor, then spotted the unmistakable form of Blair, still in his crumpled suit, standing outside the Piper, furiously waving his fist at them. He stepped out into the road, demanding that they stop. Davey slammed on the brakes, the anti-lock system drumming a frantic tattoo. Blair's face, as it grew larger in the windscreen, turned from purple with rage, to pale with concern, then white and wide-eyed with terror when he realized the big car was about to flatten him. The Land Rover shuddered to a halt close enough for him to slap a hand on the bonnet to rejuvenate his anger.

"Where the hell have you two been?" he roared, finally rediscovering the use of his legs and strutting round to the driver's side, looking slightly disappointed that he had only Davey to shout at through that window. "I told you to meet me in the pub!"

"We had a call out," Hamish said, "and now we've got a lead on two lassies linked to Gallagher."

"Well, you're no' going anywhere without me!" Blair said, yanking open the rear door to heave his bulk into the back seat. "I'm no' letting you out o' my sight, Macbeth!"

Davey gunned the engine and set off for the harbor again while Hamish explained to Blair that the two girls could lead them to Gallagher and that they were on the island across the loch.

"So we're going in a boat?" Blair asked, sounding a little apprehensive.

"I've arranged to borrow a dinghy wi' an outboard motor," Hamish said. "Room enough for Davey and me and the two girls once we have them."

"Room enough for you and me," Blair said, straightening his shoulders. "As senior officer, I will be there to arrest these two women and take them into custody. Forbes can bide wi' the car at the harbor."

"The lassies are quick and smart," Hamish said. "Maybe it would be better if—"

"I'm in charge, here, Macbeth!" Blair said, raising his voice to earache level in the confined space of the car. "We do as I say!"

Archie was waiting at the harbor with the boat. Hamish introduced Blair and Archie fussed for a minute or two, making sure Hamish knew how to start the engine, although they had been out on the loch fishing together enough times for him to know that Hamish was well able to handle the small boat.

"I would take you across myself," Archie said, "but as this is police business, I..."

"Don't worry, Archie," Hamish said, patting his friend on the shoulder, fully aware that the thought of setting foot on Whuppity Stoorie must have been filling the old fisherman with dread. "Like you said, this is police business."

He handed his cap to Davey for safekeeping, knowing that a gust of wind out on the water could easily whip it off and send it to the bottom of the loch, then helped Blair make a shaky embarkation before heading out, Blair struggling to fit a lifejacket over his suit. They said nothing for a few minutes, the sound of the engine and the steady, rhythmic clapping of waves against the bow masking even the sound of the breeze weaving its way through the surrounding mountain peaks. Blair sat with his back to Hamish, his head bowed. At first, Hamish thought the gentle movement of the boat might have rocked him to sleep, but when Blair looked round, the greenish tinge to his usually florid features betrayed the specter of seasickness.

"What are you going this way for?" Blair demanded, albeit in a rather subdued manner. "The shorter way is straight across."

"Aye, that's how it looks," Hamish said, "but we needed to sweep out to the right here. The Anstey empties into the head o' the loch, creating a constant current, and the tide is on the ebb, meaning that we could be fighting both on a straight course. The other thing is, they might be keeping a watch, but they'll no' see us coming from this direction, and I don't want them to hear us either."

With that, he cut the engine.

"From here, the currents will take us in close," he explained, "then I can restart the engine at the last minute to bring us in to the island to find a place to land. That will give the lassies the least possible warning."

"Find a place? You don't know a place?" Blair asked. "You've no' been here afore, then?"

"I've never had any reason to visit the island afore," Hamish said, deciding against giving Blair the entire tale of Whuppity Stoorie. "Nobody ever goes there. The locals think it would be... bad luck. So, apart from yon lassies we're after, it's just you and me out here."

Blair looked uncomfortable, shifted in his seat, then shuffled farther toward the bow, further away from Hamish.

"What's the matter, Blair?" Hamish asked, giving his passenger a hard stare. "Feared I might kick you ower the side?"

"I...just want this ower wi' as quick as possible," Blair grumbled.

"Well, that's one thing we're agreed on," Hamish said. "I want this business sorted out so I can get you out o' Lochdubh. I've no fond memories o' you here. How could I ever forget you pulling a gun on me, ready to shoot me, when you were doing the bidding o' those Glasgow gangsters?"

Although he had never considered fear might

cure seasickness, Hamish was fascinated by the way Blair's green tinge had now turned the faint yellowy color akin to one of those cheap lightbulbs that were supposed to last a lifetime. All things considered, Hamish mused, Blair's ability to turn from his usual tantrum red to either yellow or green made him like an overfed traffic light. He watched Blair's hand stroke a small mark on his left cheek.

"Aye, that's where the gun ended up, wasn't it?" he said. "The tables were turned and I came closer to blowing your brains out than you'll ever know. It was only your wife that saved you. Mary stopped me, or you wouldn't be sitting in this boat right now."

"Things have changed," Blair said, quietly. "That's all water under the bridge now."

"The trouble is," Hamish said, "you're never water under the bridge. You keep coming back wi' the tide like floating garbage."

"You need to watch your mouth, Macbeth," Blair said, straightening his back. "I still outrank you and you'll no' get away wi' talking to me like this when anyone else is around."

"You're right there," Hamish agreed, "so I'll

keep my temper until I can pack you off down south again. That means concentrating on the job at hand."

Restarting the engine, Hamish guided the boat into the channel that separated Whuppity Stoorie from the shore and quickly spotted a small area of rocks and pebbles beyond which a path to the trees had been freshly flattened through the ground vegetation. He cut the engine again when he was sure they were about to ground and soon heard the rumble of pebbles on the keel. Blair showed a surprising burst of agility to hurl himself out onto dry land, catching the bow line from Hamish, who then leapt ashore to secure the boat to a large boulder.

"We need to be gentle wi' these lassies," Hamish warned Blair. "They're frightened and desperate, so we need to let them know we're here to help them."

Blair grunted and nodded, and they trudged through the flattened grass to the edge of the woods. There they found the kayak hidden in the undergrowth. Hamish held a finger to his lips, urging Blair to be silent.

"If their boat's here, then they're still on the island," he whispered and pointed to his left, indicating that Blair should go that way while he circled round to the right. He looked down at Blair's footwear and was almost impressed that they were stout shoes with proper sole grips rather than city loafers. At least the man would be able to stay on his feet.

Hamish moved carefully through the wood, stepping over tangled tendrils of thorn and peering past the trees, patches of afternoon light piercing the canopy or flashing reflections from the loch through gaps in the trunks. After only a few minutes he spotted a clearing where a bright orange dome tent was pitched. On the ground by the tent, two sleeping bags were spread out and on them lay the two young women, sound asleep. He took cover behind a large oak tree.

Suddenly, from the other side of the clearing, there came a flurry of rustling leaves, the pistol-like crack of a breaking branch and a murmur of muttered curses. Hamish watched the blonde-haired girl's eyes flicker open. She gave her friend's shoulder a gentle shake to wake her, a look of alarm in her eyes. They sat up, nodded to each other and made off in opposite directions, the blonde one toward Blair, the other straight for Hamish. When she crept close enough, Hamish stepped out from behind the tree, grabbed her wrist and clicked a handcuff round it with one well-practiced movement.

The young woman squealed and tried to strike out with her free hand but he easily caught her other wrist and instantly had her fully cuffed. She struggled at first, but he held on to the cuffs with his right hand, making a calming motion with his left.

"Calm down, now, lass," he said gently. "I'm no' going to hurt you. I want to help you but I can't have your running out on me again. What's your name?"

"Kira," the young woman said, staring at the ground.

A roar of pain, more rustling of leaves and a frustrated yowling came from the other side of the clearing. Hamish led Kira in the direction of the commotion where he found Blair clinging to the other young woman's ankles. At first, he assumed Blair had executed a flying tackle to bring down his prisoner, then he noticed the tear in the knee of his trousers and the slab of stone Blair had tripped over. The young woman was struggling hard, but Blair clung on, despite the flurry of slaps and thumps she was showering on his back.

"Elena," Kira said, and her friend looked up, ceasing to struggle when she saw Kira in handcuffs. "We can't get away from the island."

"Elena, is it?" Blair said, breathing hard to pull himself to his knees. "Well, Elena, I'm arresting you for assaulting a—"

"Give it a rest," Hamish interrupted him. "Let's get these poor lassies calmed down before we have to start on all that. Kira, sit down beside Elena while we catch our breath."

He held out a hand to help Blair to his feet. Blair looked at the hand, looked up at Hamish, then resigned himself to accepting the assistance.

"Leave no stone unturned is what Mr. Farnham said," Hamish joked, bending to examine the slab over which Blair had tripped. "Well, you certainly had a go at turning this one."

He brushed a few leaves and other debris off the stone, then let out a low whistle.

"Michty me," he said, standing and scuffing his boot here and there to clear away leaf litter and undergrowth, revealing first one more stone, then another.

"What is it?" Blair asked.

"Gravestones," Hamish explained. "This is a burial ground...and look..."

He brushed some soil from the face of one of the stones, pointing out the unmistakable symbol of a skull and crossed bones.

"Pirates?" Blair frowned. "This was a pirates' graveyard?"

"No' pirates," Hamish said. "The symbol used to be fairly common on gravestones, especially for—"

"Plague!" Kira said.

"Aye, lass," Hamish said, nodding and smiling. "Your English is quite good."

"We learn at school," Elena said.

"Plague?" Blair took a step back from the stones.

"There's no' any plague here now," Hamish said, laughing. "You're more in danger o' a heart attack from all the beer and pies you scoff than you are from plague."

"But the plague was in the cities," Blair said.

"It was," Hamish said, and an image of Mrs. Roberts's classroom popped into his mind, her words during her history lesson ringing clear as a bell, "but anywhere that traded with the cities or anywhere with a harbor where ships came in from the south or from abroad was at risk. In some parts o' the Highlands and out on the islands in the fifteenth and sixteenth centuries more than a third o' the population was wiped out. Sometimes there weren't enough left living to bury the dead."

Hamish impressed himself with his recall, awarded himself the accolade of "absolute gem" in his own head, gave the gravestone one last pat and turned back to the others.

"This place gives me the creeps," Blair complained, rubbing his bruised knee. "Let's get back to the Piper. I need a drink."

Hamish crouched down in front of Kira and Elena.

"Listen, you two," he said, trying to sound

as reassuring as he could, "you've led us a merry dance, but I want you to understand that you're safe now. Nobody is going to hurt you. We'll take you back to Lochdubh and we'll work out how we can help you. The main thing is, you're safe wi' us."

"But we have done many bad things," Elena said.

"I have done a very bad thing," Kira said. "You cannot help me."

"We'll see," Hamish said. "Now come on, let's go."

He stood, held out hands to haul them to their feet, then led them to the boat.

Back in Lochdubh, Hamish and Davey sat at the kitchen table with Kira and Elena. They all had mugs of tea and the girls, now released from their handcuffs, fussed over Lugs who was overjoyed to have two brand-new friends. The two who did not seem at all relaxed were Blair and Sonsie. Blair paced back and forth across the floor while Sonsie was curled on her favorite shelf above the radiator, watching him like a security guard at a tennis match, eyes moving from left to right but her head staying perfectly still.

"We'll have to take another trip out to Whuppity Stoorie to collect the kayak, the tent and the other stuff," Hamish said to Davey. "It would be nice if we could just hand it back to the outward-bound center, but it's evidence now."

"And the island was a plague burial ground?" Davey said, sipping some tea. "That explains part of the old legend, I suppose. People would have been terrified that disturbing the remains there would cause the disease to spread again—hence the bit about Whuppity unleashing a plague."

"Aye, they'd have wanted to keep people off the island," Hamish agreed, "and ower the centuries the real reason was forgotten, but the legend lived on. Elspeth was right about yon nuggets."

"Nuggets? What the hell are you two blethering about?" Blair complained. "I thought we were going to the pub!"

Hamish stood and opened a cupboard—the same one from which Davey had produced the Glenfiddich for the seer. He was now happy that had gone—it was too good to waste on Blair. He produced a lesser bottle and put it on the table along with a glass, inviting Blair to take a seat.

"That's more like it," Blair said, pouring himself a generous measure. Now that he was stationary, Sonsie rested her eyes, quickly realized that she hadn't had a nap for almost half an hour, and drifted off to sleep.

"Ladies," Hamish said, settling back into his seat and drinking his tea, "I need you to give us your whole story, starting wi' how you came to be in this part o' Scotland."

Kira began telling how the two friends dreamed of going to New York. Elena took over from time to time, and between them they described how they had escaped from Gallagher, stayed in Mrs. Roberts's house and then encountered Kathleen Tait on the road.

"She seemed nice," Kira explained. "Offered us lift to railway station."

"But she was not nice," Elena added. "She point gun at us. She would give us back to that man!"

"So you killed her and stole her car," Blair said, taking a gulp of whisky.

"No!" cried Kira. "I mean, yes, we steal car... but..."

Kira paused, tears in her eyes, and the office phone rang, sparing her any further anguish. Davey went to answer it, but was back in the kitchen in less than a minute.

"Anonymous phone call, Hamish!" he said, interrupting Kira. "The *Millennium Falcon* has been spotted heading north from Loch Muir."

"Gallagher!" Hamish cried, grabbing his phone and calling a familiar number. "He'll be passing the mouth o' Loch Dubh afore long. We need to move fast. Archie? Aye, it's me again. We need another boat. No, your fishing boat. Aye, and you as skipper. It's urgent. Aye, we'll get you expenses..."

Davey grabbed his service belt from where he had hung it over the back of his chair and was fastening it round his waist when Blair stood up.

"Where do you think you're going, Forbes?" he grunted.

"With Sergeant Macbeth, of course. I—" Davey began, but Blair cut him short.

"You'll bide here and guard the prisoners,"

Blair ordered. "Lock them in yon wee cell until we get back."

Davey looked to Hamish, who nodded, then he ushered Kira and Elena into the station's small cell where they sat obediently on the two rudimentary single beds. Hamish rushed out to the car with Blair and made for the harbor once again.

"Are you sure you want to do this?" Hamish asked. "You didn't look too happy on the boat earlier."

"That was just a crappy wee boat," Blair argued. "I'll be right as rain on something a decent size."

Quite what Blair considered to be a "decent size" for a boat, Hamish couldn't be sure, but by the look on his face when he saw Archie's fishing boat, he was fairly certain that it didn't measure up. As far as Blair was concerned, in this instance, size really did matter. He hesitated for a few moments while Hamish fetched his tactical utility vest from the rear of the car, grabbed his binoculars and flung his cap on the front seat. By the time the big Highlander had fastened the vest in place, Blair clearly felt he was committed to another trip out on the loch. He boarded Archie's small, sky-blue boat, *Bluebell*, with a look of trepidation. At under twenty feet in length, *Bluebell* was a little less than three times longer than the dinghy they had used earlier and as soon as he set foot on deck, Blair caught a heady whiff of the diesel engine. Archie had a cigarette clamped between his lips and exhaled a plume of blue-gray smoke while rummaging in a waist-high basket to find a lifejacket that would fit Blair.

"You'll be wanting one o' these," he said, handing a lifejacket to Blair. "All my passengers have to wear one."

He looked at Hamish, wearing the tactical vest that, Archie knew, subtly incorporated body armor. He'd never seen Hamish wear one before.

"This is serious, then?" he said, tossing the lifejacket he had for Hamish back in the basket.

"Could be," Hamish grinned to show he wasn't taking it too seriously. "Come on, Archie—full steam ahead!"

Bluebell was no speedboat but she made

good headway down toward the mouth of the loch, and Hamish marveled at how different his beloved Lochdubh, slowly becoming dwarfed by the surrounding mountains, looked from out on the water. It wasn't often he took a trip to the mouth of the loch and he'd forgotten how breathtaking the mountains were when viewed from the water. He decided he ought to take Claire out in a boat to see all of this before the winter weather set in.

Bluebell's diesel engine provided a constant beat that reverberated through her wooden planks and hull, making the whole boat seem alive and mischievously playful, skimming across some of the waves but rolling gleefully over others. The sea became more choppy as they began to leave the shelter of the loch, splashing against the bow and, from time to time, the sides of the boat, sending plumes of white spray to splatter the deck. Hamish peered through his binoculars, scanning the waves ahead for any sign of the *Millennium Falcon*. He then realized that he didn't actually know what he was looking for and wouldn't be able to read the nameplate from any great distance, even if he did spy Gallagher's boat.

"Will you know Gallagher's boat when you see it?" he called to Archie, who was standing in the small wheel-house, guiding *Bluebell* with both forearms leaning on the wheel as he peered out across the Minch, the channel that separated the mainland from the islands of the Outer Hebrides. From their current viewpoint, there was no sign of the islands, the Minch looking like an endless tract of ocean, and no sign of Gallagher.

"Aye, I'll ken it, sure enough," Archie replied, turning his head at the sound of panicked footsteps on the deck behind him. Blair had scampered from the safety of the middle of the boat to the side, gripping the edge while stretching his head and shoulders as far as he dared over the water. There came a belch like a surprised frog and a violent retching.

"That was a waste o' whisky," Hamish muttered to himself, squinting into the binoculars again.

"If he chunders in my boat," Archie said, grimly, "I'll sling the bugger ower the side."

"Aye, Archie," Hamish agreed, "and I'll help you."

Hamish carried on scanning the waves, then he surprised himself with the thrill of excitement he felt when he spotted a tiny dark shape to the south.

"What about that ower there, Archie?" He pointed and offered the binoculars through the wheelhouse window. "Could that be him?"

"Might well be," Archie said, wrinkling his eyes to little more than slits but declining the binoculars. "If we keep this course, we'll be able to tell within the next few minutes."

Hamish raised the binoculars to his eyes once more, trying to steady his arm against the wheelhouse to keep the distant boat in view. He was sure he could see a trace of smoke coming from the boat, but at this distance he couldn't be sure.

"Macbeth!" Blair wailed and Hamish tore himself away from the binoculars to see the wretched sight of the DCI, kneeling on the deck, struggling out of his lifejacket. He wrestled feebly with it and, when he finally extricated himself, he held it out toward Hamish.

"Get me another one o' these," he demanded. "This one's got puke on it."

Hamish took the lifejacket from him, shaking his head in disgust at the pathetic sight of Blair huddled by the side of the boat. The older policeman's clothes were soaked with spray and vomit stains. One of his shoes had come off and, as Hamish watched, Blair loosened the belt on his trousers, rubbing his stomach.

"Oh, my guts," Blair groaned, then looked up at Hamish. "Well don't just stand there gawping! Get on wi' it!"

Hamish made his way to the stern where he dropped the lifejacket in a plastic bag Archie clearly kept for passenger litter. It would have to be retrieved and cleaned up later. Somehow, given that Archie regularly took holidaymakers out in his boat, he doubted this was the first time a lifejacket had suffered this indignity. He then danced forward, balancing along the heaving deck to the basket full of lifejackets and was rummaging through them when Archie called out.

"We've got a better view o' him now!" Archie

announced from the wheelhouse and Hamish looked up, pressing the binoculars to his eyes. "I think that's him all right, Hamish!"

Hamish steadied himself against the wheelhouse once more and had just managed to train the glasses on the target boat when he heard more thunderous retching from Blair's direction. He lowered the binoculars, picked out a lifejacket and turned to toss it to Blair, but he couldn't see him. He quickly checked round the other side of the wheelhouse and looked down into the small hold, but there was no sign of him. Then he heard a screech of terror and looked out over the stern to see Blair thrashing around in the water.

"Oh, bloody hell!" Hamish gasped, then yelled to Archie. "Archie, turn round! Blair's gone overboard!"

He stripped off his tactical vest, unclipped his service belt and swiftly removed his boots, all the time keeping his eyes fixed on the spot where he had seen Blair, who had now disappeared. Then, when a wave lifted the struggling figure back into sight, Hamish dived over the side. The shock of the cold water made him gasp when he broke the surface and he knew he couldn't afford to be in the sea for long. The cold would quickly sap his strength and in the waters around this part of Scotland's coast, hypothermia could begin to set in within minutes. Blair, he knew, would be in an even worse state. He'd been flailing around, wasting his strength, and he was in pretty poor condition physically. If Hamish couldn't get him back on the boat fast, he'd be dead.

"Blair!" he yelled, swimming out of a trough and gaining a better view when the wave lifted him higher in the water. He spotted Blair just a couple of yards away, struggling to the surface after having been engulfed by a wave. "Blair! I'm here!"

Hamish swam closer and Blair, coughing out seawater, grabbed hold of him, trying to cling on.

"No!" Hamish yelled at him. "Calm down! You can't—"

Then a wave washed over them and he found he was being dragged under by a panicking Blair. They were both submerged and Hamish, gasping for air, pushed the DCI away from him.

He knew the frantic Blair would drown them both unless he could get him to stop thrashing about. He broke the surface, took in a huge gulp of air, could see no sign of Blair and then forced himself back under the water. The saltwater was stinging his eyes and visibility was poor. He could see little more than an arm's length. Then he felt something—the sleeve of Blair's jacket. He clutched at it, then grabbed Blair's arm and kicked hard for the surface. As soon as his face was out of the water, Hamish sucked in a desperate gulp of air. With it came a swallow of sea-water. Coughing up the water, he made sure Blair's face was above the surface and cursed when he realized that the man was no longer struggling—he wasn't moving at all.

Kicking hard with his legs to keep them both afloat, Hamish was looking all round to see if he could spot Archie in *Bluebell* when an orange lifebelt hit the water near his head. *Bluebell* was just a few yards away and Archie was standing on deck, holding the rope that was attached to the lifebelt. Hamish grabbed the lifebelt and dropped it over Blair's head, reaching down to heave his arms up through the ring. The effort left him all but exhausted, although Blair was now safely wedged in the lifebelt. With a surge of relief, he felt the ring start to move toward *Bluebell*. He clung on as Archie hauled on the rope, drawing them to the side of the boat.

Hamish grasped a rope dangling from *Bluebell*'s side, watching Archie hoist Blair far enough up the side of the boat to keep his head clear of the water.

"Archie," Hamish gasped. "I can't hold on much longer..."

A short aluminum ladder suddenly appeared, Archie clamping it to the side of the boat. Hamish slung an arm over the lowest rung, griping it with his armpit. He reached for the next rung with his free hand but his fingers were now cripplingly cold and, try as he might, he could neither grip with his hand any longer, nor kick with his legs. He felt his hold on the ladder beginning to slip, and then his wrist was caught in a crushing grip. He looked up to see Archie reaching down the ladder, his fingers clasped around Hamish's wrist.

"Come away, now, laddie," Archie said, staring Hamish in the eye. "I'm needing your help here."

With Archie's support, Hamish fought his way a little higher up the ladder, then managed to get first a knee, then a foot on the bottom rung. A moment later, he collapsed onto the deck, panting with effort as though he'd just run up every mountainside around Loch Dubh.

"There's no time for that," Archie said, slapping Hamish on the back. "I need you to help me get your pal out o' the water."

Hamish shook his head, clearing water from his eyes and ears, then crawled to Archie's side.

"Grab an arm!" Archie yelled above the sound of the waves and the engine. "We can't let him drop out o' the ring!"

Together they pulled Blair up out of the water and he tumbled over the side of the boat onto the deck. There he lay, unmoving. Archie leaned over to take a look at his face.

"I reckon he's snuffed it," was all the old man said.

"No," Hamish gasped, now utterly exhausted.

"No, he can't be…They'll blame me…They'll take my station away…my home…No!"

He lunged across the deck, balanced both hands on Blair's chest and began counting chest compressions. Then he tipped Blair's head back, pinched his nose and breathed air into his mouth. He repeated the process again and again but there was no response. Screaming with anger as he felt the very last of his strength drain from his body, he slammed his fist down on Blair's chest and collapsed on the deck beside him.

"You bastard, Blair…" he breathed.

At that moment a gush of water erupted from Blair's mouth. Archie immediately rolled him onto his side and thumped him on the back whereupon Blair coughed up more seawater than Hamish thought it possible for any body to have absorbed. He then gulped in huge groans of breath, coughed and spluttered some more before his eyes finally opened. He propped himself up on one elbow, staring with bleary eyes at Hamish. Archie helped him into a sitting position against the side of the boat and then produced warm, dry blankets from the engine room, wrapping them around both Blair and Hamish. He also handed them cups of hot, sweet tea from a Thermos flask.

Hamish shivered, sipping his tea, and Archie promised to have them back ashore, warm and dry in no time.

"We'll have to let Gallagher's boat go," he said, "but by the way yon smoke's coming off his engine, I doubt he'll be going far."

Blair looked across at Hamish, now sitting on the deck beside him, then looked away again. They drank their tea in silence until Blair looked round again.

"I dreamt you were snogging me," Blair said, weakly. "Kissing me, full on the lips."

"No tongues, though," Hamish replied, so relieved to be out of the water, warming up and heading home that he almost managed to laugh. "Your dream, my worst nightmare, believe me."

"And what's this?" Blair said, lifting his blanket slightly to look underneath. "Where's my breeks?"

Hamish now noticed for the first time that Blair had no trousers.

"You must have lost them in the water—nothing to do wi' me!" Hamish said, and this time he did laugh. "Hurry up and get us back to Lochdubh, Archie, afore he has me up on some kind o' sexual assault charge!"

Archie looked round, gave a lopsided, closed-mouth smile that carefully failed to reveal his lack of teeth, then turned back to his course, satisfied that his passengers were recovering.

"Back there in the water—I thought I was going to die," Blair said, swallowing hard.

"I think that, for a wee minute, maybe you did," Hamish replied.

"I ken what you did, Macbeth, and I'm right grateful," Blair said. "You saved my life."

"Don't go ower the side again," Hamish warned, shaking his head and smiling. "Next time maybe I'll no' bother."

"Thank you, Macbeth," Blair said, holding out a hand to Hamish. "I owe you."

Hamish looked Blair straight in the eye and saw nothing of the blustering, bullying bigot he had come to know and detest over the years. Could coming so near to the end really have changed him? Surely he couldn't shrug off years of backsliding and double dealing in the matter of a few minutes just because he'd had a close shave? Maybe not, but if it kept him on his best behavior in the meantime, so much the better. He reached over and shook Blair's hand.

Chapter Eight

There is a wisdom of the head, and...
there is a wisdom of the heart.
    Charles Dickens, *Hard Times* (1854)

By the time *Bluebell* drew alongside her berth
in Lochdubh harbor, Hamish was feeling much
recovered, although still cold and tired. He was
surprised that Blair, although he needed help
to disembark, was able to stand unaided on the
quayside. Archie had phoned ahead and the local
GP, Dr. Brodie, was waiting for them. He made
both Hamish and Blair sit on a convenient bench
while he quickly checked them over.

"Mr. Blair, I think we should get you to the
hospital in Braikie," he said, "just to be on the
safe side."

"No hospital," Blair grumbled, sounding far

more like the DCI Hamish knew and loathed, before giving a surprise offering of gratitude. "Thank you for your concern, doctor, but all I really want is to get to the hotel, get warmed up and get to bed."

Dr. Brodie looked at Hamish, who shrugged.

"Silas will make sure he has everything he needs," he said, "and keep an eye on him overnight."

"Very well," Dr. Brodie said, "I'll take Mr. Blair directly there and speak to Silas. Now what about you, Hamish?"

"I'll take care of him," said Davey, stepping forward and immediately noting Hamish's look of alarm. "Don't worry about our two guests. They're locked up safe and sound. Let's get you home."

Davey drove back to the station and Hamish went directly upstairs to the bathroom. He walked straight into the shower, standing under the hot water fully clothed. He looked down at his socks and noticed a toe poking through on his left foot. He'd have to darn that before it got any worse. He suddenly felt disproportionately elated that he'd taken off his boots before diving into the sea. The saltwater might well have ruined them. They were good boots. They'd see him through the coming winter for sure. Why was he thinking like this? Why was he thinking of such trivial things when he and Blair had nearly died out there in the Minch? Probably, he decided, because he wanted to push all those darker thoughts out of his mind. He considered that to be the best thing to do right then and stripped off his clothes, throwing them out of the shower into the bathroom sink and concentrating on when he'd get a chance to put them in his washing machine. Maybe not tonight.

He dried himself off, suddenly felt overcome with fatigue and crawled into bed. He was asleep within seconds.

The following morning, Hamish woke to the smell of breakfast cooking and swung himself out of bed feeling remarkably well rested and ready to take on another day. Once he'd washed and dressed, noticing that his sea-soaked clothes had gone from the bathroom, he glanced out of his bedroom window to see an ambulance parked outside. He rushed downstairs to see Claire standing in the kitchen, dressed in her green paramedic uniform. She burst into tears and flung herself at him, wrapping her arms around him.

"Archie told Davey all about it," she said, sobbing. "What were you thinking o'? You put your life on the line for Blair! How could you do that?"

"How could I no'?" Hamish said, gently stroking her hair. "Come on now, lass. I couldn't let a man drown if I had the chance to help him. It's what we do, is it no'?"

Hamish looked across to where Davey was standing wearing a floral apron over his uniform, distracted from tending the food in the pan on the stove. Kira and Elena sat at the kitchen table, eating the previous batch of sausage-and-egg rolls. All were looking in his direction.

"Morning, ladies," Hamish said. "Mind you don't burn my breakfast, Davey, I'm half-starved without any supper last night."

"Well, there's no' much wrong wi' you if

you're thinking about your stomach," Claire said, straightening her uniform and smiling up at him. "I've got to get back to work. Charlie's waiting in the van outside. I'll see you later. No more heroics today, all right?"

"I'm ay ready for a nice, quiet day," Hamish said, and stooped to kiss her goodbye.

When Claire left, Hamish sat at the kitchen table with Kira, Elena and Davey, chatting as they all finished their breakfast.

"So you came from Riga in Latvia," Hamish said. "What's it like there?"

"Not like here," Kira said. "Riga has river and many beautiful buildings, but no mountains."

"Do your families know you're here?" Davey asked.

"Our families live out in countryside," Elena said. "We go to Riga to find work."

"We want work," Kira assured them, sounding agitated. "We don't want to steal."

"Aye, all right, calm down, lass," Hamish said. "We saw you both working in the Piper. We know you'd rather work than steal. Did you have jobs in Riga?"

"We both worked in market," Elena said. "Is where we met. People think we are sisters. Maybe we are more like sisters than any other family now."

"Yes, sisters," Kira reached out to hold Elena's hand.

"We worked hard in market. Saved money to go abroad," Elena explained. "We met people there who promised us many things. We paid them much money."

"You know, you could have come here without paying to be smuggled into the country," Davey said.

"We did not want to come here," Kira insisted. "We were promised visas and to work as models in New York!"

"But first we must work here to pay for next stage of journey," Elena added.

"Now we think next stage would never happen," Kira continued. "They cheated us. They would make us work and never let us go."

"Maybe," Hamish said, looking from Kira to Elena with a solemn expression. "Exactly what kind o' work did they have planned for you?"

Kira's eyes narrowed, a swell of anger flushing her face.

"Not what you think!" she snapped. "We are not sex workers! We would rather be dead..."

"Aye, okay," Hamish said, calming her down. "You're both young and hard workers, so there are plenty other jobs they could have found for you to make money out o' you."

There came a knock at the back door and it was pushed open a little, Blair's head popping in for him to scan the room. He was never sure what to expect in this place. The lunatic dog was bad enough but the savage cat was to be avoided at all costs.

"They'll be out down the beach," Hamish said. "It's safe to come in."

"Fine, aye..." Blair said uncertainly. "I'm no' worried. Just checking."

"Are you all right to be up and about?" Hamish asked, noting that Blair was wearing a suit identical to yesterday's, but with trousers.

"Aye, yon doctor Brodie came to see me this morning," Blair said, with a puzzled frown. "Said I'd be fine if I took it easy and told me to get down to breakfast and have a good fry-up. Have you ever heard a doctor prescribe that afore?"

"Brodie's ay been like that," Hamish said. "He likes nothing better than tucking into a big plateful of everything the health nuts say you shouldn't eat."

"Aye, well it set me up a treat," Blair said, patting his stomach. "So now we need a plan to catch up wi' Gallagher."

"Kira, Elena," Hamish addressed the girls, "I need to have a wee chat wi' my colleagues, so I'll have to ask you to step back into your room."

"Not room—prison cell," Kira said.

Hamish gave her a smile of apology and guided them back to the cell before returning to the table where Davey was filling a mug of coffee for Blair just as Jimmy Anderson arrived. Davey went to the cupboard for another mug.

"Davey told me all about yesterday," Jimmy said. "I can't believe we got so close to Gallagher and then lost him."

"I don't think he got very far," Hamish said. "Archie reckoned his boat's engine was on its last legs."

"There's an alert out for his truck," Jimmy

said. "If he tries to take any road out o' Sutherland, we'll get him."

"Right now we need to agree what we do wi' Kira and Elena," Hamish said to the two senior officers. "I don't have the facilities to keep them here much longer. That cell's no' up to much and there's only a wee washroom attached."

"They could still have plenty to tell us that will help us find Gallagher," Blair said. "If we hand them on now, we might lose access to them altogether."

Jimmy looked at Blair, uncertain what to make of his old adversary. Blair had once been his boss, before Jimmy had been promoted to the same rank, and Jimmy had never trusted him. They had even come to blows more than once. He couldn't ever remember Blair looking so calm or sober.

"You're right," he agreed. "If they're passed on to me in Strathbane, they'll be processed through the system, the immigration people will get involved and we'll have to jump through all sorts o' hoops just to say hello to them."

"We'd best keep them here, then," Hamish said. "We'll look after them."

"Right," Jimmy said, draining his coffee and

standing up. "My boys have come up wi' a couple o' leads in Braikie and a few names in Inverness—people who had dealings wi' Gallagher. I doubt it will come to anything, but I want to be in on the interviews."

"We'll start putting the word out about the boat," Hamish said. "If he had engine trouble, he must have had to put in somewhere. We'll take a drive up the coast and ask around."

"I need to update Farnham," Blair said, looking at his watch. "I'll walk back to the hotel."

"You? Walk?" Jimmy said in disbelief.

"Aye, I walked all the way here earlier and..." Blair chatted casually to Jimmy as they left the station.

"That's a turn up for the books," Hamish said. "I doubt I've ever been in a room wi' those two afore when there hasn't been either swearing or punches thrown."

"Uncle Jimmy's mellowed since he gave up the drink," Davey said. "Maybe Blair's changed, too, after his near-death experience."

"I have serious doubts that will last..." Hamish mused.

*　　*　　*

Hamish was dealing with some paperwork when a call came through on the station's landline.

"Lochdubh police station," Hamish said, lifting the phone to his ear.

"The *Millennium Falcon* has foundered on the Dragon's Teeth," said a voice, and the line went dead.

"Davey!" Hamish called. "We've had another one o' those anonymous—"

When Hamish loped through to the kitchen, he found Davey standing staring at the back door and there, in the doorway, was a woman Hamish judged to be a couple of years older than Davey, with short, dark hair and dazzlingly blue eyes. The woman reached into her handbag, fished out a small, black wallet and flipped it open to show Hamish a warrant card.

"DS Susan Meadows," she said, smiling politely. "I'm here to talk to Constable Forbes."

"Aye, of course," Hamish said, buckling his service belt. "I have to go. You can use the front office, DS Meadows. Dave...um...Constable

Forbes, there's been a sighting o' the *Millennium Falcon*. I have to go. I'll pick up DCI Blair along the way. Mind we have those prisoners."

"The *Millennium*...?" DS Meadows looked confused.

"It's a long story," Davey said, moving toward the office. "We can go in here."

Hamish couldn't be sure but, as he climbed into the Land Rover, he cast a glance through the office window to where Davey and DS Meadows were sitting at his desk, and it looked very much like she reached out to place her hand gently on his.

"What the hell kind o' an interview is that?" he muttered to himself, then busied himself with phoning Blair to make sure he was ready to go.

DCI Blair was, indeed, ready and waiting when Hamish crunched to a halt on the gravel outside the Tommel Castle. He hauled his bulky frame into the passenger seat and Hamish sped off down the drive. By the time they were crossing the Anstey, he was talking to his contact at the Coastguard.

"Aye, we got a call, too, Hamish," came the

voice from the car's speaker system. "There's an S-92 inbound from Stornoway. Alistair Murray's your man."

"Thanks, Paul," Hamish said. "I'll listen out for him."

Hamish raced round the loch, turning off the road after a few minutes onto a track that wound its way uphill onto a headland that looked out over the Minch.

"Ooooh," Blair groaned at the sight of the water. "I've seen enough o' the sea to last me a lifetime."

"You'd best bide in the car when we get there, then," Hamish said. "We've no' far to go now. The Dragon's Teeth are a collection o' muckle rocks at the foot o' a wee cliff. If Gallagher or anyone else is still on yon boat, we need to get them out o' there."

The track Hamish was following ended in an open area, surrounded by gorse and heather, that was clearly used as a car park but he drove straight past all the empty parking spaces to a narrow gap that the Land Rover barely squeezed through. They were then driving across a flat area of grass, which swept off to the right into more gorse and heather on a slope that rose toward a distant, unseen mountain peak. To the left, the grassy plateau ended abruptly at what was clearly the lip of a cliff. Hamish stopped the car and jumped out, dashing over to the very end of the grass and staring over the edge. He then turned and hurried back.

"It's Gallagher's boat all right," he informed Blair, raising his voice to be heard above the sound of the wind whistling across the clifftop, "and it's being battered to bits down there on the rocks!"

"Any sign o' him?" Blair asked.

"Not so far," Hamish answered, and rushed to the back of the car where he opened the tailgate and, moments later, reappeared wearing a bright orange survival suit.

"In the name o' the wee man!" Blair declared. "You're no' thinking o' going back in yon water, are you?"

"No' if I can help it," Hamish said, just as the car's radio crackled.

"Coastguard to Lochdubh One," came the

voice and Hamish grabbed the radio handset from the dashboard.

"Good morning, Alistair," Hamish said, leaning clear of the car and cupping a hand to his ear. "I can hear you out here somewhere but I can't see you."

"We're right here, Hamish," came the voice and the grassy plateau was suddenly engulfed by the roar of two mighty engines and the thunderous drumming of rotor blades as a huge Sikorsky helicopter rose up from beyond the cliff edge. The aircraft, resplendent in red-and-white HM Coastguard livery, filled the windscreen of the car, inciting Blair to cower against the seat back.

"Ay the one for a grand entrance, Alistair," Hamish laughed, watching the helicopter drift gracefully sideways and slowly settle on the grass thirty yards from the car. The winchman at the open side door waved and signaled for Hamish to approach.

"Are you seriously going to let them lower you down to yon boat?" Blair was appalled. "Have you done this afore?"

"I train wi' the rescue lads," Hamish yelled

above the helicopter's din. "I've done this hun-dreds o' times!"

Actually, three times would have been more accurate, but he wasn't about to let Blair know that. Crouching, although he'd been told many times it wasn't strictly necessary, he ran toward the helicopter and accepted the white helmet offered by the winchman. Wearing it, he could now talk to the pilot and crew direct.

"Eric will be taking care of you today, Hamish." Alistair's voice filled Hamish's helmet and the winchman gave him a "thumbs up." "We can get you down there to check for signs of life, but if it gets at all dodgy, we're hauling you out."

"Agreed," Hamish nodded and Eric fastened a harness round him, clipping it to the winch cable along with his own.

Blair watched from the car as the helicopter lifted from the ground, the downdraft from its rotors flattening the grass while the lift those spinning wings generated dragged the enormous bulk into the air. To Blair it looked like a gigan-tic, red-and-white bumble bee—as if it shouldn't be able to fly, yet somehow it could.

Hamish was perched on the very edge of the side alongside Eric, their legs dangling through the doorway. He now got his first real look at the *Millennium Falcon* and it was not a pretty sight. Although it sat upright, pinned sideways against the Dragon's Teeth rocks by the force of the waves, juddering and swaying every time the larger waves pounded its side, the boat was beginning to list. Like Archie's boat, it was built of wood, although it looked big enough to take two *Bluebell*s on its deck. The deck itself was tilted at an angle toward the shore and there were scorch marks around what Hamish took to be the engine hatch. The hold cover was absent and, had it not been for the fact that the boat was listing away from the rushing waves, it would surely have filled with seawater. The wheelhouse structure, larger than *Bluebell*'s, had partly collapsed and the side door was hanging off its hinges.

"Here we go, Hamish," Eric said, and he swung away from the side door on the winch cable, taking Hamish with him. From having all his weight on his bottom when he was sitting in the doorway, Hamish suddenly found himself supported by the harness, his torso feeling heavy but his legs seeming light and somehow redundant. The winch lowered them slowly down to the deck, where Hamish's feet touched the wooden planking first. His knees buckled slightly when his legs took his weight once more and, in a heartbeat, Eric was standing beside him.

"We have to stay on the winch," Eric said and Hamish nodded.

"I want to see in the hold," Hamish said and they inched toward the void in the deck. Hamish took a torch from his pocket to shine into the darkness but there was nothing but water and debris sloshing around in the bottom of the hold. From where they now stood, Hamish had a better view of the wheelhouse and through the side door could see what looked like the sleeve of a jacket on the floor.

"The wheelhouse!" he called to Eric. "Looks like someone's in there!"

Just then the boat lurched sideways and the angle of the listing deck became precariously steep. There was a crack of splintering wood and it was clear that the *Millennium Falcon* was breaking up.

"That's it," Eric said. "We're out of here."

"No!" Hamish yelled. "There's someone in the wheelhouse!"

He reached for his harness and unclipped it, dashing toward the broken wheelhouse door. A torrent of words from both Alistair and Eric, which were even further from accepted radio etiquette than their usual banter, assailed Hamish's ears. Reaching the door, he yanked it aside and looked into the wheelhouse to see nothing but a discarded black jacket lying inside. Then the boat rolled sideways and Hamish went from standing on the deck to lying on his back across the now horizontal wheelhouse doorway. He began to panic when he was drenched by a fountain of spray. His heart pounded with dread at the thought of ending up back in the water again. He'd never survive being battered against the rocks or crushed by the hull of the boat.

He scrambled to his feet, balancing on the wheelhouse and immediately felt an almighty blow knock him off his feet. He felt himself fly through the air and looked down to see Eric's legs wrapped round his waist. Quick as a flash Eric clipped Hamish's harness back on the winch while delivering a string of obscenities that culminated in him slapping Hamish's helmet and howling, "You total eejit!"

There was silence for a few seconds as the winch began hoisting them back up to the helicopter's side door, then came the sound of Alistair and the rest of the crew laughing.

"That's the most swearing I've ever heard anyone do without drawing breath!" Alistair said. "Hamish, you owe Eric a big drink! Come to think of it, we're a crew of four and you owe us all a big drink!"

There was a loud cheer from the whole crew, then Alistair guided the aircraft back onto the grass plateau and set it down gently on the same spot as before. Hamish handed the white helmet back to Eric and apologized. Eric grinned and made a drinking gesture with his right hand. Hamish smiled, nodded and trotted back to the Land Rover.

"Did you see anything down there?" Blair

asked, watching the helicopter heading out across the sea back to Stornoway. "What happened?"

"Nothing much," Hamish said, nonchalantly peeling off the survival suit. "Fairly routine, really."

"Aye, right," Blair said. "If yon was routine, give me a Saturday-night punch-up in Glasgow any time you like."

"The thing is," Hamish said, settling himself in the driver's seat, "Gallagher wasn't on board. That means he either went ower the side like we did and he's now at the bottom o' the Minch, or he abandoned ship in some kind o' dinghy."

"He's got the luck o' the devil," Blair grunted. "He's still alive and well somewhere around this miserable wasteland."

At that moment, Hamish knew the old Blair was still lurking somewhere inside that crumpled blue suit. They drove back down to the loch road in silence, then Hamish posed a question to Blair.

"There was a female DS came to talk to Davey just afore I left," he said. "Was that anything to do wi' you?"

"Nothing that I ken about," Blair said. "Maybe something to do wi' the trouble he got into in Edinburgh."

"What trouble was that?"

"I'm no' entirely sure," Blair said, chuckling. "Some kind o' sexual shenanigans. The punishment was coming to work wi' you again."

"Well, I'm glad to have him," Hamish said, scowling at Blair. "Davey's a good policeman."

"Aye," Blair said, a wave of good nature washing over him once more, "maybe he is."

They made it back to the station without indulging in any further conversation, Hamish contemplating what he would put in his report about the *Millennium Falcon* incident and what Alistair and his crew would put in theirs. The drink he had promised them would ensure they left out anything about his moment of madness, but it was probably worth a phone call to Alistair to get their stories straight. He was still thinking about it when he walked into the kitchen where Davey was sitting with a cup of tea.

"Where's DS Meadows?" Hamish asked.

"She's gone," Davey said, looking as guilt-laden and remorseful as a puppy caught chewing your favorite socks.

"More to the point," Blair barked, flinging open the door to the cell, "where are the two prisoners?"

Davey leapt to his feet and charged into the cell, scarcely able to believe his eyes.

"How did they get out?" Blair demanded, his face flushed with fury.

"I thought you locked the cell door," Davey said, turning to Hamish.

"No, I just put them in there," Hamish admitted, running his hand through his hair. "We were all sitting here, so it didn't seem necessary to lock them up."

"So they just strolled out!" Blair roared. "They wandered out without you or this DS Mellors—"

"Meadows," Davey corrected him.

"Don't you dare interrupt me, laddie!" yelled Blair. "How did they get past you and this female DS? Sneak off upstairs together for a shag, did you?"

"You can't say—" Davey stepped toward Blair with fire in his eyes, but Hamish was quicker, grabbing his arm and pointing out through the front window.

"Your car's gone from the street," he said. "They must have taken it."

"Then they won't get far," Davey said. "When I arrived here the tank was empty. I was running on fumes. I'm surprised it even started."

"Get out there and find them, now!" Blair ordered. "I've done enough chasing around today for a man that actually died yesterday. I'll wait here and…"

Attracted by the commotion, Sonsie appeared outside the kitchen window, fixing Blair with the unsettlingly wide stare of her yellow eyes, baring her tiger-like teeth and hissing like blood on a barbecue.

"On the other hand," Blair said, with a sudden change of heart, "maybe a wee walk back to the hotel will do me good."

Hamish and Davey took the Land Rover along the shore road and within a couple of minutes spotted Davey's car parked outside the church.

They drew up in front of it and got out to take a look around, the first to catch their eye being the formidable figure of Mrs. Wellington, the minister's wife, standing on the church doorstep. She was a woman of substantial proportion who wore tweed outfits that made a kind of rustling noise when she walked. Hamish always found that vaguely irritating, being of the impression that your clothes really shouldn't be making any noise at all.

"Sergeant Macbeth!" called Mrs. Wellington. "I think you'd better come inside."

Hamish and Davey walked up the path to the church and followed Mrs. Wellington down the aisle. There, sitting in the front pew, were Kira and Elena.

"What are you two doing here?" asked Hamish. "I told you we would help you. We can't do that if you go running off first chance you get."

"This is church," Kira said. "We come here for sanctuary."

"Here we are safe," Elena added.

"Sergeant Macbeth," Mrs. Wellington said,

standing between Hamish and the girls and folding her arms, a gesture to which her tweed jacket objected with more of a creak than a rustle. "It is outrageous and completely morally unacceptable that you two male officers are staying overnight in that tiny police station with these two vulnerable young women."

"Mrs. Wellington," Hamish began to explain, "these two young women are key to a serious crime investigation."

"Would that be the murder over near Scourie?" Mrs. Wellington asked.

"Who told you that?" asked Hamish.

"How many other serious crime investigations are you conducting right now?"

"Fair point."

"It is unacceptable that they should stay with you," Mrs. Wellington went on. "I therefore propose that you release them into my care."

"That would be most irregular, Mrs. Wellington," Davey pointed out. "We can't take the risk that they will abscond again."

"They will not attempt to escape," Mrs. Wellington assured Davey. "They have both pledged a vow at the altar here that they will remain with me until such time as you make other arrangements for them."

"Aye…" Hamish pondered. "That might just work. You would have to keep a keen eye on them, though, Mrs. Wellington, and let us know if they disappear."

"We will not disappear," Elena promised.

"I will not let them," Mrs. Wellington maintained.

"Very well," Hamish said, turning to Kira and Elena. "Remember, ladies, we *will* find you if you run away and you'll then have to go to a proper prison."

"We will stay here, Sergeant," Kira said. "We will not go."

Hamish and Davey drove up to the Tommel Castle Hotel to break the news to Blair that Kira and Elena were safe and secure. As they turned into the driveway, Davey looked a little anxious and began a conversation as if to ease his nerves.

"DCI Blair will be glad that we still have Kira and Elena," he said.

"Aye," Hamish agreed, then wondered about

it, "or maybe no". He seems to swing from being a reformed character back to being the old Blair again in the blink o' your eye."

"He's like Jekyll and Hyde," Davey said.

"Jack and who?" Hamish asked.

"*Strange Case of Dr. Jekyll and Mr. Hyde*," Davey explained, "was a novella written by Robert Louis Stevenson in 1886. Dr. Jekyll was a scientist who..."

To Hamish's amusement, Davey then delivered a rapid-fire lecture on Stevenson's book that lasted until he parked the car and would have continued had Hamish not then told him to, "Wheesht!" He wasn't sure why Davey was feeling nervous, but he didn't need him babbling away when they talked to Blair.

At the reception desk, the hotel manager, Mr. Johnson, told them that DCI Blair had looked very tired and had gone to his room to rest with instructions that no one was to disturb him. Hamish decided it was in their best interest to honor those instructions and they turned to leave.

They were halfway down the front steps when Priscilla appeared, calling sweetly to Davey.

"Back again?" she said with the captivating smile she knew men couldn't resist. "What could it be about this place that you find so irresistible, Davey?"

"Ah, Priscilla," Davey said. "I really don't…"

"I know," Priscilla said, touching the Police Scotland badge on his chest, "you don't have time right now because you're on duty and working terribly hard but you must come up for that drink later."

"I'm away to send Blair a text message," Hamish said, walking to the car.

"Priscilla, the thing is…" Davey removed Priscilla's hand from his badge and as he talked, Colonel George Halburton-Smythe watched unseen from the entrance hall. He watched the young policeman reject his daughter's advances and saw his daughter become visibly upset. This would never do! It was bad enough that something might have been going on between them, but it was intolerable that he should reject her. She should be the one to do the rejecting! It had been utterly humiliating when Macbeth had spurned his precious Priscilla, he wasn't letting another common-or-garden plebian police woodentop get away with it!

"Now see here, you young scoundrel!" the colonel called, marching down the stairs. "The likes of you does not get to give my daughter the brush-off! If there's any brushing off to be done, she will be the one doing the brushing!"

"Oh, for goodness' sake, Father!" Priscilla wailed, pushing past him, her head down and a wobble in her voice. "Maybe it's time I went back down to London."

"Sorry," Davey said, and walked swiftly over to join Hamish in the car.

"What was that all about?" Hamish asked, heading back to the station.

"It ... it was nothing, really," Davey replied.

"And your wee visit from DS Meadows—was that nothing, too?" Hamish gave Davey a look that let him know his patience had run out. "Come on, Davey. What's going on?"

"Let's get back to the station, Hamish," Davey said. "We can sit down and I'll tell you the whole story."

Chapter Nine

It has often been remarked of the Scottish character, that the stubbornness with which it is molded shows most to advantage in adversity.
  Sir Walter Scott, *Old Mortality* (1816)

"How much do you know?" Davey asked, sitting at the kitchen table in the police station. Hamish put a mug of tea in front of him that bore the image of an overweight policeman snoozing in a hammock and the slogan, "Easy PC."

"Assume I know nothing," Hamish said, joining Davey at the table with his own steaming mug. Lugs padded over to the table and dropped his head in Hamish's lap, hoping for any morsels of food that might come his way. Sonsie was still outside on the window ledge in the sunshine,

276

possibly awake. "That's what your Uncle Jimmy told me—nothing. That's pretty much what Blair told me—nothing. So it's fair to say that, apart from what's been bubbling away in my own imagination, I know nothing."

"Then I'll start from the beginning," Davey said. "When I left here last time and went down to Edinburgh, I was flung into the thick of things. There was a lot of work and every shift was full-on. I ended up working extra hours just about every shift, unpaid, just to keep up with the paperwork."

"That's no' so unusual for a young police officer," Hamish said.

"You're right," Davey agreed, "and I'm not complaining, but the shift patterns meant that I started to spend a lot of time with...certain colleagues...and I became...involved...with one of them. We knew it was a bad idea and we tried to call a halt to it. We even changed shifts so that we could keep each other at arm's length. Then, one nightshift, we were both in the station, things were quieter than usual and the place was pretty much deserted. One thing led to another, we kissed and then we ended up...you know... making love."

"Who was this colleague you couldn't resist?" Hamish asked.

"My sergeant," Davey said.

Hamish raised his eyebrows.

"You've met her," Davey explained. "She was here—DS Meadows."

"You and her," Hamish said, "in the station. I'm taking it you found a quiet spot?"

"The inspector's office." Davey hung his head, unable to look Hamish in the eye. "The inspector was out and wasn't expected back."

"And someone walked in on you?" Hamish guessed.

"Our inspector," Davey nodded, "found us there, on the desk."

"Och, Davey, Davey, Davey..." Hamish rubbed his eyebrows, covering his face with his hands as though horribly perturbed by the story, but actually shielding a huge grin that he could no longer contain. He felt poor Davey's pain, but there was an enormously funny side to the story. It was like seeing someone slip and fall flat on their backside. It's not funny in itself, and it's painful and embarrassing for the person who falls, but you can't help finding it funny because it's someone who's lost their dignity—and you laugh because you're relieved it wasn't you. Sadly, it would take Davey a long time to pick himself up off his backside and see anything funny in the situation.

"You were caught in the act on your inspector's desk by your inspector!" Hamish said, pulling a serious face and dropping his hands. "I'm guessing your father was furious when he heard about this,"

"Not as furious as my auntie," said Davey.

"What's your auntie got to do wi' it?"

"She was our inspector."

"She...what?!" Hamish could control himself no longer and burst out laughing. Davey slumped back in his chair, holding his arms out in exasperation.

"You see," he said, plaintively, "this is why I don't like to..."

"Okay, I'm sorry, Davey," Hamish said, bringing himself under control, "but you got yourself in a right pickle there, didn't you? What happened next?"

"There was a hell of a stramash," Davey said. "At one point we thought we were both going to be sacked. Then we were told we could keep our jobs if we accepted disciplinary action. We'd be returned to uniform and transferred. They wanted to keep it all low profile—as little fuss as possible. They were terrified the press would turn it into some kind of police sex scandal story."

"I have to say, your wee problem worked out well for me," Hamish admitted. "I got you back here."

"And I was glad to come here," Davey said. "I love it up here and my father thought it would be a good place. Uncle Jimmy's close by and I'm far enough away from Edinburgh to keep any scandal rumors to a minimum."

"What about Sergeant Meadows?" Hamish asked. "She still identified herself to me as a DS and she wasn't in uniform."

"It still says detective sergeant on her warrant card, just like it still says detective constable on mine," Davey said. "She's on leave. She's working

out of a wee station just north of Perth. I didn't
know she was coming. It's the first time I've seen
her since..."

"But I'm guessing it's no' going to be the last,"
said Hamish, shaking his head and smiling.
"Auld Angus was right, wasn't he? Love blossom-
ing out o' the shame, or whatever it was he said.
This was more than just a fling, wasn't it?"

"That was almost scary," Davey said. "The seer
certainly saw right through me. In a way, he even
helped me decide what I need to do. The thing is,
Susan and I want to be together. She's had enough
of the job. She wants to leave and retrain as a teacher.
This is real, Hamish. I want to be with her."

"Those are things the pair o' you need to work
out carefully," Hamish advised, "but whatever
you decide, you'll ay have my support, Davey—
and I'll no' say a word to anyone about—"

Hamish paused when his phone rang. He
became tense as he listened, sitting up straight,
promised he'd "be there right away" and rang off.

"Mind on the job, Davey," he said, getting
quickly to his feet. "Hector says Gallagher just
paid him a visit."

They raced out to the Land Rover and roared off in the direction of the Piper where Hector was waiting for them by the side of the road. Davey lowered the window and Hector, looking slightly shaken, pointed toward the bridge over the Anstey.

"He went that way," Hector said. "Blue pickup truck."

Davey nodded a *thank you* and Hamish urged the Land Rover forward as quickly as he could make it go. When they crossed the humpback bridge, they hit the crest so fast that the big car lifted all four wheels off the ground, landing with a jolt in time for Hamish to power it round to the right to begin the climb toward the main Strathbane road. They came across just one car in front of them and when Davey switched on the blue lights, it pulled over to allow the police car to speed past.

When they reached the junction with the main road, Davey looked out to the left where the road snaked off into the distance across the moorland.

"We'd see him if he'd gone that way, Hamish," he said, but Hamish was already turning right.

"Aye, he's heading south toward Strathbane," he said. "Get Jimmy on the phone, Davey. He'll get everything available up on the road."

While Davey spoke to his godfather, Hamish concentrated on keeping his speed through the twists and turns of the narrow road. Thankfully, there was very little traffic and what vehicles they did encounter were heading toward them, the drivers gawping as the big Land Rover with its flashing lights thundered past.

"There he is!" Davey said, catching a fleeting glimpse of Gallagher's truck rounding a bend up ahead before the road took it through a clutter of rocky outcrops where it immediately disappeared again.

"Aye, that must be him," Hamish agreed, keeping his right foot as hard on the accelerator as he dared. Moments later, they reached the same bend and rock formations, hurtled round it to find a long, straight stretch of road with Gallagher's truck dead ahead. There was a small puff of smoke from the pickup's exhaust and it began to speed up.

"He's seen us!" Davey said.

"Aye, but we're still gaining on him," Hamish replied, and within a few seconds they were barely twenty yards behind. Suddenly, Gallagher's truck veered across the road, narrowly missing an oncoming car that swerved violently to avoid a collision.

"Is he totally nuts?" Davey gasped.

"No," Hamish said grimly. "He's trying to do what he did to the lassies in Tait's car. He knows if he forces somebody to crash, we'll have to stop."

With that, Gallagher jinked toward an oncoming car, a small, green hatchback, side-swiping it and sending it spinning off into a roadside expanse of bracken and heather. Hamish immediately slowed down, watching the blue pickup disappearing into the distance and slapping the steering wheel with frustration.

"We have to see if anybody's hurt, Davey," he said, turning the Land Rover and heading offroad toward the green car. Davey jumped out and ran to the car once they were close. The middle-aged couple inside were pale with shock but otherwise uninjured. Their car's suspension, however, had collapsed at the front and the vehicle was undriveable. Hamish then saw the first car Gallagher had tried to wreck coming back down the road. Clearly they wanted to bear witness to the madman's driving. Hamish knew he and Davey were going to be there for quite some time and gazed off in the direction Gallagher's truck had taken. Their only hope of catching him now was if Jimmy could get his people on the road before Gallagher turned off onto one of the many side roads and tracks between there and Strathbane. In all likelihood, however, Gallagher had escaped their clutches once again.

It was later that afternoon when Hamish and Davey finally returned to Lochdubh. They called in at the Piper and Hector shook his head angrily when he saw them walk in.

"No' in here!" he breathed, trying not to attract attention from the few customers in the bar but attracting every eye in the place nevertheless. "You lads are seriously bad for business. Come round to the office."

Hector's office was little more than a store

room off the kitchen, made all the smaller by having three large men crowd into it all at once. There seemed to be a little more breathing space when they all sat down, Hector taking the chair behind a rickety table he used as a desk.

"Is this about Gallagher?" Hector asked.

"Good guess," said Hamish, his facetious tone irritating the old boxer. "What did he come to see you about?"

"Yon lassies," Hector said, placing his giant paws on the table and shaking his head. "Somehow he'd heard that they'd been working here and he was boiling mad about it."

"Was he angry with them or with you?" asked Davey.

"Both," Hector said. "He accused me o' tempting them to work for me. I never tempted them—they just showed up! Then he went mental about them costing him a fortune if he couldn't find them. He said something about passing them on to someone who was willing to pay good money. He made them sound like…"

"Slaves," said Hamish, gravely. "Real human beings, real people, but to him just another commodity he's smuggled. Did you tell him where they were?"

"I've no idea where they are," Hector said. "Last time I saw them, you were chasing them out o' my kitchen and leaving me wi' a right old mess to clear up."

"Aye, sorry about that, Hector," Hamish said. "They can be a bit o' a handful, yon pair."

"Well, I never want to see them again!" Hector said. "The last thing I want is the likes o' Mick Gallagher showing up in my pub!"

"Do you know if he went anywhere else in the village?" Hamish asked.

"I saw him cruising up and down the road out there in yon truck o' his," Hector said. "I was about to phone you when he pulled up outside here. Then I had to wait till he had gone afore I could speak to you."

"Don't worry, Hector," Hamish said, standing to leave. "I'm pretty sure we'll have Gallagher in custody afore too long."

Back at the police station, Hamish and Davey waded through the mountains of paperwork generated by the mayhem Gallagher had created up on the Strathbane road. Jimmy called to let them know that none of his people had been able to find any trace of Gallagher's blue pickup truck.

"Here's a funny thing, though," Jimmy said. "Blair has invited me, you and Davey for dinner at the Tommel Castle Hotel this evening. He's picking up the bill."

"That's no' like him at all," Hamish said, "but I'm no' turning down an offer like that."

"I'll see you there, then," Jimmy said. "Seven-thirty. Don't be late. I want to get back to Strathbane at a decent hour."

"Jimmy," Hamish said, catching his old friend before he could hang up and checking to see that Davey was in the kitchen, boiling the kettle for more tea. "Davey told me about what happened in Edinburgh."

"Oh, he did, did he?" Jimmy replied, then gave a rasping laugh. "It's no' really funny, but on the unofficial Police Scotland gossip circuit he's become some kind o' legend! The story gets a wee bit more outrageous wi' every retelling. There was even a whisper that it involved the chief constable's desk!"

"It will take a while for all that to die down," Hamish said, "but eventually the gossips will move on to something else. They always do."

Hamish had rung off by the time Davey came into the office with the tea. He wasn't so enthusiastic about dinner at Tommel Castle.

"Is that because o' Priscilla?" Hamish asked.

"Well…yes," Davey confirmed. "I mean, I know now that I want to be with Susan, but I was a bit taken with Priscilla at one time. The thing is, she seems to think that I would always be at her beck and call. She liked to flirt but it was all about making her feel like the most desirable creature on the planet. She never really seemed to want to give anything back."

"Aye, you're spot on there, Davey," Hamish said, laughing. "I tried to tell you afore, but…"

"I know," Davey said. "I should listen to you more often. I don't want to run into her or her father again any time soon. I'll stay here and mind the station."

"Drop in on the manse as well," Hamish said, "just to make sure the girls are all right wi' Mrs. Wellington."

"Aye, I'll do that," Davey assured him.

Hamish spent the rest of his time on the paper-work wondering which of Freddie's delicious creations he would sample for dinner that evening. When he thought of the coffee-marinated roast venison saddle, his stomach rumbled and he took that as confirmation from his belly that that's what he should order. You should never argue with your belly.

Arriving at the hotel that evening wearing his best suit, the one that Claire always liked to point out was his only suit, Hamish was greeted by Mr. Johnson, who told him that DCIs Blair and Anderson were awaiting him in the dining room. Hamish checked his watch. He was bang on time. Jimmy must have been even more keen for a free meal than he was.

"Macbeth!" Blair gave him an effusive welcome. "Come in and sit down, laddie. What would you like? A beer maybe? A wee dram? Order whatever you like, I'll be picking up the tab."

Hamish ordered a lime juice and soda,

determined to keep his wits about him. He looked across the table at the beer in front of Jimmy

"Non-alcoholic," Jimmy said, tapping the glass. "No' as good as the real thing, but no' bad nowadays."

Blair had opted for a whisky and took a swig before leaning into the table and lowering his voice so that the diners at the three other occupied tables couldn't hear.

"You're probably wondering why I asked you both to dinner," Blair said.

Hamish and Jimmy looked at each other, then at Blair.

"I reckon Hamish is just like me," Jimmy said. "We've been wondering about nothing else since you called. It's no' like you to splash your cash about."

"This will all go on expenses," Blair said, dismissing the thought that he might pay for it with a wave of his hand. "Anyway, I thought it would be a good idea for us all to compare notes and see where we can go from here…" He paused for a moment, looking round as though he'd lost something. "Where's young Forbes?"

"He's manning the station in case we get any more calls about Gallagher," Hamish said, "and trying to trace the anonymous calls we got about Gallagher's boat."

"He's a hard-working lad when he puts his mind to it," Blair said, nodding. "A credit to his family, Jimmy."

Blair stopped to blow his nose and Jimmy looked at Hamish, raising his eyebrows. This didn't sound a bit like the Blair he had come to know and hate.

"So—what about suspects for Kathleen Tait's murder, Jimmy?" Blair said, tucking his handkerchief into the breast pocket of a gray suit that looked to Hamish like it had been freshly pressed.

"As far as I'm concerned," Jimmy said, "we still have all o' the MacDougalls on the suspect list, including Shona. They all have motive—Tait had stolen Shona's husband and they wanted revenge. They might even have tried to force Tait to tell them where Gallagher was. We now have the pathologist's report and the cause of death was strangulation. The marks on the neck suggest that the murderer didn't have particularly big hands, so it may have been a woman. None o' the MacDougalls have alibis that we can verify—together or separately, they're all suspects."

"If it could have been a woman," Hamish said, "then Kira also has to be a suspect. We know she was at the scene around the time o' the murder and she definitely has a motive—she and Elena were being held at gunpoint, they were facing an uncertain future and they wanted to make a run for it."

"What about Hector MacCrimmon?" Blair asked. "He keeps cropping up in the midst o' all this."

"He does," Hamish agreed, "but he has hands like a gorilla and I don't see how he had a connection to Tait."

"Let me fill you in on that—" Blair started to talk, then his phone rang. "Bloody hell! Can a man no' get a minute's peace to speak?!"

He slammed his fist down on the table, rattling their cutlery and causing the surface of their drinks to tremble in their glasses, creating miniature tsunamis. The other diners frowned in their direction and Blair stood, pressing his phone to his ear and marching out of the dining room.

"He's acting very strange," Jimmy said.

"Like Jekyll and Hyde," Hamish agreed.

"Like who?" Jimmy tilted his thin face to one side like an inquisitive fox.

"It was a book by Robert Louis Stevenson," Hamish informed him. "Davey told me all about it. When nice Jekyll drank a wee potion, he turned into nasty Hyde. Davey said it was about the duality of human nature, and the Victorian obsession with presenting an unimpeachably respectable public appearance and the societal dichotomy that was created when some fine, upstanding public figures were living a degenerate, sinful life in private."

"Did he really, now?" Jimmy said. "Maybe his parents didn't waste all that money on an expensive education after all—but what does it mean?"

"It means that Blair now seems to be a good cop and bad cop all rolled into one," Hamish said.

"He was easier to deal wi' when he was just a straightforward bad cop," Jimmy decided.

Blair returned and dropped into his chair.

"That was Farnham," he said by way of apology. "The man's constantly on my back for updates. Where were we?"

"Suspects," Jimmy reminded him. "The final one, of course, is Michael Gallagher. He was at the scene, he was in cahoots wi' Tait and he's known to have a violent temper."

"We don't know why he would want to kill Tait, but I'm pretty sure we'll find a motive once we get him in custody. In the meantime, we also want him for assault, enough smuggling and fraud counts to fill a whole book o' charge sheets, and people trafficking, as well as speeding and reckless driving," Hamish added. "He'll be going to prison for a long time … if we can ever find him."

"Right," Blair said. "Well, at least I can fill you in a bit on him now. Afore, when it looked like we might pick him up easily, Farnham wanted this all kept under wraps. Now, he says I should tell you everything—anything that might help find Gallagher."

"About time," Jimmy grumbled and there

was a further short interruption when the waiter came to take their orders. Hamish and his belly were delighted to find that the venison was on the menu.

"Gallagher and Tait were partners down south," Blair explained, leaning into the table and lowering his voice again. "At that time they were known as Michael Price and Karen Hill. They were both involved wi' a lot o' dodgy gangland characters and they were present when a man named Dan Cochrane was murdered. They eventually handed themselves in and told us everything. They helped us put away some major gangland villains in return for immunity and protection. They were given new identities so they could start new lives."

"We'd already figured out that much," Jimmy said, sounding distinctly unimpressed.

"We thought you might have," Blair admitted. "Gallagher and Tait were keen to take the deal because they were friends wi' the murdered man and they had been working wi' him to steal from the gang that murdered him. Basically, they were skimming profits from various rackets and when the gang found out, they sent in the heavies to deal wi' them.

"Gallagher's mate was killed but he and Tait got away because he took out a couple of the bruisers. He's no' that big but he's a black belt in just about everything. He was a cage fighter known as Mighty Mouse. That's how he originally got talking to Hector MacCrimmon. They were both in the fight game."

"So Gallagher and Tait were a couple?" Hamish asked.

"Aye," Blair said. "Partners in crime and in every other respect."

"Then why did Gallagher marry Shona Mac-Dougall?" Hamish wondered.

"Gallagher and Tait were no' supposed to see each other anymore," Blair said. "To make their new identities work, they agreed to split. Farnham warned them they'd get no more support from the program if they didn't stay apart and they needed that support for just about everything from bank accounts to National Insurance numbers or even registering wi' a dentist. Later, they did seek each other out and it would appear they started getting up to their old tricks again, handling stolen goods and the like. Seems they also progressed to smuggling. We think Gallagher married MacDougall to throw Farnham off the scent—make him think he'd fully adopted his new life when, in fact, he was still seeing Tait."

"What's your role in all this?" Hamish asked.

"I got dragged into this just to spot potential bad lads like Hector MacCrimmon," Blair said, "and the sooner I can get back to normal the better."

"How does any o' that help us find Gallagher?" asked Jimmy.

"It doesn't," Hamish said. "No' on its own, anyway, but it tells us a bit more about what kind o' man he is. He's definitely a risk taker. We also know he wants to get his hands on Kira and Elena. I'm beginning to think they could be key to us getting our hands on him."

It had grown dark by the time Hamish was polishing off the cranachan he had ordered for dessert, and back at the police station Davey was sitting in the small living room with Lugs and Sonsie for company, having enjoyed a steaming plate of mince, tatties and peas for supper. He jumped to his feet when the station phone rang and rushed through to the office to answer it.

"Lochdubh police station," Davey said, holding the phone to his ear.

"You're not Sergeant Macbeth," came the voice of Nessie Currie.

"Sergeant Macbeth," echoed Jessie in the background.

"No, he's not here right now," Davey explained. "This is Constable Forbes."

"Well, I suppose you'll have to do," Nessie said, making no attempt to mask the disappointment in her voice.

"Have to do," came her sister's despairing repetition.

"What can I do for you, ladies?" Davey asked.

"We were closing our curtains when we looked out toward the churchyard and saw a graverobber!" cried Nessie.

"A graverobber!"

"You know," Davey said patiently, "graverobbers are really a thing of the past. It doesn't happen nowadays."

"Then he must be after the lead off the church roof!" Nessie decided.

"Chu-u-urch roooof!" Jessie chanted, managing to sound like an angel banished from a heavenly choir. Nessie hung up.

Davey grabbed his service belt, remembered that he had a good flashlight in the pocket of his tactical vest and reached for that, too. He knew Hamish seldom wore his vest and thought he would follow suit, fumbling for the flashlight in a pocket. A second or two later he changed his mind, deciding it was easier just to wear the vest, and shrugged it on.

The churchyard lay between the old church and the manse and it took Davey only a couple of minutes to jog along there to check out the Currie twins' report. He found his flashlight as he walked past the churchyard gate and switched it on, the powerful beam cutting through the darkness to illuminate row upon row of headstones. When he played the beam around the graveyard, it looked almost as if the old stones were moving, such was the way their shadows lengthened and shrank. Then he spotted one shadow moving against the others. Someone was there!

"Stop! Police!" Davey shouted. "Stay right where you are!"

He picked out a figure with his flashlight and whoever it was immediately froze. Davey kept the light on the figure, walking closer to see that it was a man dressed in a black sweater and black trousers, facing away from him.

"Turn round," Davey ordered and the man slowly turned toward him. Once his face was in the light, Davey instantly recognized the man from the photos that James MacDougall had provided. It was Michael Gallagher. He looked to be no more than about five feet, nine inches tall and his slight stature gave Davey no cause for concern. He felt excited. He would be the one who finally apprehended the elusive Michael Gallagher. The man's face had the look of a viper about to strike but Davey was undaunted. He now had Gallagher cornered and was relishing the prospect of slapping cuffs on him.

"You're a hard man to find, Mr. Gallagher," Davey said, "but I've got you now, so don't make this difficult for yourself."

"This'll no' be difficult for me, son," Gallagher said, and shot forward, his right leg flicking out with the speed of a lightning strike. His foot caught Davey in the chest, sending him reeling backward.

Davey had just regained his equilibrium when Gallagher was on him again, throwing a punch that Davey dodged, managing to land one of his own on Gallagher's forehead. Gallagher staggered back, tripped on a headstone and tumbled to the ground. Davey made to pin him down, reaching for his handcuffs but Gallagher bounced straight back to his feet, delivering a flurry of punches to Davey's head which landed in such quick succession that Davey reeled off to the left, dropped his flashlight and was forced to steady himself on a monument to regain his senses. The flashlight landed on a grave at such an angle that its wide beam pointed upward, illuminating the scene.

Gallagher leapt forward and Davey tried to push him aside but the smaller man reached to his belt and swiped his hand out in an arc. Davey felt a searing pain in his right arm, heard a dragging sound as something scraped across his utility vest, then felt the same, horrendous, burning pain in his left arm. Both arms dropped to his sides and he glanced down to see blood coursing down onto his hands. Gallagher had pulled some kind of knife.

Gallagher gave a coarse laugh and then launched a punch that left Davey sprawled across a gravestone. He advanced on the helpless young police officer, then heard a voice shrieking from somewhere out in the darkness.

"You! You there in the churchyard! We can see what you're doing!" cried the voice. "We can see you!"

"See you!" came a shrill echo.

Gallagher looked down at Davey's unconscious form, then turned and ran, disappearing into the night. Davey lay still and silent, bathed in the glaring beam of his flashlight and bleeding profusely.

Hamish was enjoying a particularly fine Italian coffee and wondering when Blair, who had been

Dr. Jekyll almost all evening, might next turn into Mr. Hyde when his phone rang.

"Sergeant Macbeth!" came the voice of Nessie Currie. "Your Constable Forbes is in the churchyard and he's been in a fight!"

"Been in a fight!" Hamish heard Jessie repeat in the background.

"Can you see him?" Hamish asked, jumping to his feet. "Is he moving?"

"He's not moving," Nessie informed him, "and there's a lot of blood."

"A lot of blood!"

"I'm coming," Hamish said and hung up, turning to Jimmy. "It's Davey, Jimmy! He's hurt bad!"

Hamish sprinted out to the Land Rover, jumped in and shot off down the driveway. Jimmy and Blair, not quite so quick on their feet, followed moments later and took Jimmy's car. Hamish was at the churchyard in less than two minutes, where he met Dr. Brodie hurrying through the gate carrying a medical bag.

"You got a call?" Hamish asked, running up a path between the rows of headstones toward a bright light.

"Aye, the Currie twins," Dr. Brodie replied, breathing hard. "Look! There he is."

They found Davey where Gallagher had left him, slumped over a gravestone, bleeding from the deep cuts at the tops of his arms.

"Davey!" Hamish called, kneeling down beside his friend. "Talk to me, Davey!"

He kept talking to Davey, repeating his name, trying to coax a response, but all Davey could manage was a few groans. Dr. Brodie and Hamish moved Davey into a position where the doctor could better assess his patient's condition. He and Hamish knelt either side of Davey.

"I'd say he was concussed," Dr. Brodie advised, seeing the bruising on Davey's face, "but these cuts are the biggest problem. He's lost a lot of blood." He produced two packets from his medical kit, tearing them open and removing two large dressings. He handed one of the dressings to Hamish.

"We have to try to stop the bleeding, Hamish. Hold this on the wound, apply pressure and keep his arm raised."

They were each dealing with one of Davey's arms when Jimmy and Blair arrived.

"Davey…" Jimmy breathed.

"We need an ambulance!" Dr. Brodie called to Jimmy.

For an instant, both Jimmy and Blair appeared to freeze.

"Do it, Jimmy!" Hamish roared and Jimmy whipped out his phone.

Chapter Ten

O Whisky! soul o' plays and pranks!
Accept a Bardie's gratfu' thanks!
Robert Burns, "Scotch
Drink" (1785)

Dr. Brodie battled to stabilize Davey and by the time an ambulance pulled up outside the church-yard, he had managed to control the bleeding. Claire and her crew-mate, Charlie, had made sure they were the first medics on the scene, Claire having driven like the wind when she heard over the radio that a police officer had been stabbed in Lochdubh. They rushed over to lend a hand, Charlie helping Dr. Brodie while Hamish stepped back, staring at Davey, unable to take his eyes off him for even a second.

"He'll be okay, Hamish," she said, putting

an arm round him and resting her head against his shoulder. "We'll get him to Braikie now and they'll be able to take care of him properly there."

"The cuts are deep," Hamish said, quietly. "He's lost a lot o' blood."

"He's young and strong," Claire said. She quickly wiped her eye, not wanting anyone to see a trained paramedic, on duty, crying, yet unable to stem the tear she was ashamed to have shed through relief that it was Davey on the ground in front of them and not Hamish. She now felt guilty for having had that thought. "He'll get through this."

She reached up to kiss him on the cheek, then went to help Charlie set up an intravenous drip and move Davey onto a wheeled stretcher to take him to the waiting ambulance. Hamish walked alongside the stretcher, still staring at Davey's bruised and battered face. Then Davey's eyes flickered open and he looked up at Hamish. His lips moved. Hamish leaned closer and Davey whispered one word.

"Gallagher."

Hamish nodded in response. A surge of anger boiled inside him but he clenched his fists, forcing himself to stay calm, his eyes fixed on Davey.

"Don't worry, Davey," he said. "Concentrate on getting better. I'll take care o' Gallagher."

Claire and Dr. Brodie went in the back of the ambulance with Davey and Jimmy followed on in his car, insisting on going to the hospital with his godson as Davey's parents would never speak to him again if he didn't. Both Claire and Jimmy promised to keep Hamish informed about Davey once they reached the hospital. Hamish was left at the churchyard gate with a gaggle of locals who had been distracted from the evening's TV viewing by the flashing lights. Hamish advised them all to go back home, then spotted the Currie twins.

"It was a smaller man who did that to Constable Forbes," Nessie said. "He was dressed in black."

"Dressed in black," said Jessie, somberly.

"Did you see which way he went?" Hamish asked.

"Just disappeared into the darkness," Nessie said. "He was very quick, but Constable Forbes punched him in the head—knocked him down."

"Knocked him down," Jessie agreed.

"Thank you, ladies," Hamish said. "Without you we might not have got to him in time. You've been . . . absolute gems."

He said goodnight and was watching them march proudly home together when Blair approached him.

"He's a fit young laddie," Blair said. "He'll be okay."

"He better be," Hamish growled, "or I'll make sure Gallagher never lives to see the inside o' a prison cell."

"We have to catch the bugger first," said Blair.

"Aye," Hamish replied, looking up toward the manse where Mrs. Wellington was standing at the front window, flanked by Kira and Elena. That was what had brought Gallagher back here. He must have spotted them at the manse when he came in to talk to Hector and come back to check out how he might spirit them away.

"I've an idea we're wasting our time chasing after Gallagher, trying to catch him. Maybe we need to make him come to us."

Hamish gave Blair a lift back to the hotel, then called Elspeth and asked her to meet him in the bar. He ordered himself a whisky, she chose the same and they sat at the end of the bar where they would not be overheard. News that there had been some kind of incident near the church had reached the hotel, but the village rumor mill had been bereft of detail and Elspeth had been in her room, undisturbed by any of the gossip.

"What would you say if I was to tell you the name o' the woman murdered ower near Scourie?" Hamish asked.

"I'd say these drinks are on me!" Elspeth smiled, placing a hand on his arm. From the grim look on his face and the thinly veiled anger, she didn't need her second sight to tell her that something was wrong. "What happened tonight? You seem really out of sorts."

Hamish explained how Davey had cornered a man in the churchyard and that the man had cut

311

him badly with some kind of knife. Elspeth was horrified.

"What if it had been you?" she said. "If you'd been the one to confront him, you wouldn't have been wearing the Kevlar vest—you never do."

"I need you to help me catch this man," Hamish said.

"Of course!" Elspeth replied. "I'll do anything. How can I help?"

"The woman who was killed is Kathleen Tait," Hamish said. "I can give you the details if you can make sure it goes out on the lunchtime news tomorrow."

Hamish drove back to the police station with thoughts about Davey's churchyard confrontation reeling in his head. If only he could have been there, too. If only Davey had called him before going there. If only...Anxious for news about how Davey was doing, he had his phone in his hand as he walked into his kitchen, about to call Claire, when Jimmy rang.

"How is he?" Hamish asked before Jimmy could say a word.

"He's going to be okay," Jimmy replied. "He's going to be out o' action for a while. He's got a broken cheekbone, he's concussed and he's going to need surgery on his arms to repair muscle and tendon damage, but the people here are telling me he'll make a full recovery. If you and Brodie had no' got to him when you did, it might have been a different story. As it is, he's going to be fine."

"That's a relief," Hamish said, taking a seat at the kitchen table and fending off the over-enthusiastic welcome from Lugs and Sonsie. "It was Gallagher, Jimmy. I'm fed up chasing after the bastard. Now we have to nail him. Here's what I want to do..."

He was still sitting at the kitchen table an hour later, going over the plan in his head, brooding and sipping whisky, when Claire walked in.

"Hamish," she said, standing in the doorway, eyes wide. "I thought it was you!" She walked into his open arms and he held her close, feeling her rush of love chase dark thoughts of Gallagher to the back of his mind.

*   *   *

The following morning, Hamish visited Davey in Braikie Hospital. Walking along the windowless corridor to the ward where Davey had been put in a side room, he decided he was all too familiar with the sights, sounds and smell of the place. The heels of his boots squeaked on the polished linoleum and the flat, artificial lighting made it difficult to tell if it was day or night.

Davey's room, thankfully, had a window, although the blinds were drawn. When he walked in, Davey turned his head on the pillow, and gave a feeble smile.

"Hamish," he said weakly. "Open those blinds for me. The place feels like a dungeon if I can't see the sky."

Hamish immediately did as he was asked, then took a good look at Davey. The bruising on his face had taken on dark, livid colors of blue and green, contrasting with the redness of the scuffs and grazes. His arms were immobilized and heavily bandaged, and the bedclothes were stretched and tucked up to his armpits tighter than a new shoe. Clearly, the nurses who had directed Hamish to Davey's room did not want their patient moving about.

"How are you feeling?" Hamish asked, sitting in the bedside chair.

"Much better since Uncle Jimmy left," Davey said, holding on to his smile. "He was hanging about here like a corpse at a wedding."

"He's no great liking for this place," Hamish said. "He was in here himself after his car crash."

"I'm still a bit woozy about what happened last night," Davey said, "but I can remember two things. It was Gallagher. He was quick. He was hitting me so fast it was like I was being attacked by a gang…but I got one good hit in on him."

"Aye, the Currie twins said they saw you deck him," Hamish said. "They were the ones who called me and Dr. Brodie. Without them…"

"I owe Nessie and Jessie a big thank you," Davey said. "I'll pay them a visit as soon as I'm back at work."

"And I'll have you back as soon as you're ready," Hamish said, "but not afore then. I want you fit and able."

"I'll be back," Davey said, "don't you worry about that."

They chatted for a while longer before Hamish realized that he needed to be elsewhere. His plan to snare Gallagher was about to start falling into place. He was making his way along the corridor when he saw DS Meadows walking toward him, her face pale with concern. He nodded a brief greeting.

"He's going to be all right," was all he said, before she whispered a trembling "Thank you" and rushed to Davey's room.

In the Loch Muir Inn, Albert was behind the bar, polishing glasses and watching the TV news on the big screen. Half a dozen of his regular lunch-time customers sat at a couple of tables, arguing about the football over the weekend and coming to their usual conclusion that all referees were of questionable parentage.

When the news anchor announced that they were going over to Elspeth Grant and the picture switched to an image of her with the Lochdubh police station in the background, she attracted a few admiring glances and a couple of calls of, "Aye, look—there she is!" The pretty local girl who had made it onto TV as a reporter and newscaster was always given an appreciative, if proprietorial, welcome when she appeared on screen. The locals all liked to think that she was still one of them, that she belonged to them, as a way of sharing in her success.

"Here in Sutherland," Elspeth said, "the mystery surrounding the identity of the murder victim whose body was found in a house in the Scourie area has now taken a new twist. Local police have confirmed that the name of the victim is Kathleen Tait . . ."

Albert's face froze. He stared at the screen but heard neither the rest of Elspeth's report, nor any of the rumble of conversation from his customers. He put down the glass he had been cleaning, tossed the dish towel aside and reached under the counter.

"Here you go, lads!" he shouted, standing bottles of premium Scotch whisky on the bar. "The last o' the good stuff. Think o' it as a closing down sale—it's all on the house! Help yourselves!"

For a heartbeat, there was complete silence, then there was a huge cheer and a mini-stampede for the bar. Albert left his jubilant customers pouring each other drinks and slunk off through a door to the kitchen.

Minutes later, with his customers downing large measures, he climbed into his truck and set off up the Glenmuir road. He didn't get far. He turned a corner to find Hamish's Land Rover blocking the narrow road. He slammed his truck into reverse, looked over his shoulder and saw the lanky figure of Hamish Macbeth striding toward him. Albert switched off the engine and slumped over the wheel. He knew he couldn't escape and, a couple of seconds later, Hamish wrenched open the car door.

"Hello, Albert," he said, noting the suitcase on the passenger seat. "Thinking of taking a wee holiday, were you?"

"I was just going to … um …" Albert mumbled.

"Well, we can talk about where you were just going shortly," Hamish told him. "Right now, you're going back down to the Loch Muir Inn. You're going to send your customers home and shut up shop properly. First, step out o' the car."

Hamish searched Albert, confiscating his phone, then took his suitcase and ordered him back into the truck.

"There's enough room for you to turn round, just back there," Hamish said, pointing to a field entrance. "When you get to the pub, you'll find your telephone landline's no' working and you've no internet, since that comes via your landline. Tell the customers to get out. Do not breathe a word to them about me being here. I'll be out o' sight and I'll be watching them leave. Do as I say, everything will work out just as I want it to and I'll go easy on you. If things don't work out as I want, you'll be charged wi' so many offenses it'll take me all day to read them out. Those offenses will include being an accessory to kidnap, attempted murder and murder."

"Hold on a wee minute," Albert said, frowning at Hamish. "I can't be charged wi' that. There's no such thing as being 'an accessory' in this country."

"Very good, Albert," Hamish gave him a thin

smile. "I'm guessing you've had a few barstool lawyers chatting in your pub ower the years. There's no 'accessory.' That's just an easy way of saying that you were 'art and part' o' the crimes. In Scotland, that carries the same prison term as the crime itself. Do you understand? I can help you, if you help me, but if I even think you're no' playing nicely, you'll spend the rest o' your days in a prison cell."

"If I tell you anything," Albert said, "and Mick's friends find me, it's no' a prison cell I'll be in, it's the bottom o' a peat bog!"

"I've got news for you, Albert," Hamish advised him. "Gallagher's no' got any friends. Those that used to know him now want him dead, and you as well if they think you're one o' his pals. All I need do is whisper a word or two in the right ear and they'll find you, whether you're in prison or no'. Getting involved wi' Gallagher was the worst decision o' your life. Now you've got nowhere to turn to except me."

"All right," Albert said with a heavy sigh. "I'll get the punters out o' the pub."

Albert returned to the Loch Muir Inn and

Hamish parked his car out of sight behind Mrs. Roberts's house, his old teacher delighted to be involved in a police operation with one of her old pupils, even if she was ordered to stay indoors until it was all over. Hamish watched the road, counting the vehicles leaving the Loch Muir's car park. When he was sure everyone had gone, he walked down to the inn. Albert was clearing glasses from tables.

"Force o' habit," he said. "I ken I'll never be opening up here again, but at least I can leave things tidy."

"Do you own this place, Albert?" Hamish asked.

"No chance," came the reply. "It's owned by some businessman in Edinburgh. He says he wants to turn it back into a country house one day but he hardly ever sets foot in the place. I'm just the manager."

Hamish took a seat at one of the freshly cleaned tables and invited Albert to sit opposite.

"So how did you get tangled up wi' Gallagher?" Hamish asked.

"He came in here one day, offering me cheap whisky," Albert answered. "It was ay good stuff and the real McCoy—none o' your fake knock-offs."

"You must have known he was bringing it in from abroad."

"Aye, that was part o' the deal. I helped him land the goods. It was no' always whisky. He brought in some perfume and even cigars and tobacco."

"And the girls?"

"Aye, that was a new thing," Albert said, shaking his head. "I never wanted any part o' that and neither did Kathleen, but Mick was no' the sort o' person you could argue wi'. He kept control o' them by hanging on to their passports. He had customers that he passed his 'passengers' on to and they paid good money."

"Does he still think he can get good money for Kira and Elena?"

"Those two led him a merry dance. Kira picked his pocket for their passports and his wallet, but he's got them back again now. I think it's no' just the money wi' any o' his passengers. He can't afford to disappoint his customers. They're the kind o' people who are liable to rearrange your kneecaps if you let them down."

"Did Gallagher land all of his cargo here?"

"Aye, it's a nice quiet spot. Even when there are people on holiday, camping nearby, nobody pays any attention to a wee boat coming in off the loch. Anglers do it all the time when they've been night fishing."

"That could be risky if they spotted you."

"Part o' my job was to make sure the coast was clear. He'd then anchor the fishing boat out in deeper water and bring in the dinghy."

"What if the coast wasn't clear?"

"Then he would bring in the dinghy and pick me up as if we were off for a spot o' night fishing. There's an auld boathouse farther up the loch. It hasn't been used since this was a big house. The only track that goes down there collapsed into the loch in a storm years ago, so you can't get any kind o' car down there. Sometimes Mick used to park in the woods off the Strathbane road and hike ower the hills to reach the boathouse, but you couldn't take any goods out that way. We would leave stuff there until it was safe to bring it in to the beach. It's easy to get a truck or a four-wheel drive in here."

"How did you contact him?"

"By phone, although I never actually phoned him. He spent so many years being battered about the head in the fight game that he doesn't always hear so well. He likes text messages."

"Show me," said Hamish, handing Albert the phone he had taken from him. Albert called up the list of text messages between the two men and Hamish studied it for a few minutes. There was a succession of messages, Gallagher's to Albert short and gruff, while Albert's to Gallagher were a little more wordy. There were no greetings or sign-offs and nothing frivolous or jolly. They didn't use text symbols, abbreviations or emojis but typed their texts almost as though sending old-fashioned telegrams. Hamish took out his own phone and hit a speed-dial number.

"Okay, Jimmy," he said. "Bring them all in."

A few minutes later, Jimmy Anderson arrived with Kira and Elena. They looked less than delighted to be back in the Loch Muir Inn and were accompanied by a female police constable. They were followed by Blair with Shona, her father and brother. Hector MacCrimmon walked in behind them.

"What's this all about?" Andrew MacDougall demanded.

"I told you that you would want to be here for this," Hamish said, "but you're going to have to be a wee bit patient, so make yourselves comfortable in the meantime."

"I've got officers up on the main road and hiding out o' sight on the Glenmuir road," Jimmy said. "Any sign o' Gallagher and they'll let me know."

"Good," Hamish said, "but I suspect he'll no' be out and about on the roads."

He approached Kira and Elena, and pulled a handful of plastic cable ties out of his pocket.

"I know it must be difficult for you being back here," he said gently, "but we need to catch the man who brought you here in the boat."

Kira looked toward Albert.

"The other man," Hamish said. "He is dangerous. He hurt Constable Forbes very badly. I need to put these around your wrists so that we can take a photograph. Once we have the photo, we will cut them off."

"Constable Davey is nice," Kira said, holding out her wrists.

"We hope he is better soon," Elena added, offering Hamish her wrists, too.

Hamish positioned the girls by the bar and held up Albert's phone to take their picture.

"Should I be in the photo, too?" Albert asked.

"Don't be daft," Hamish chuckled. "You're meant to be taking this picture, Albert. We don't want you in it and a selfie would be weird."

With the photo taken, Hamish cut the cable ties and directed Kira and Elena to sit at a table with the female officer. He then sent a text message to Gallagher using Albert's phone.

I have the girls.

Hamish took a seat, praying that the message would be answered. Everything depended on Gallagher thinking Kira and Elena were in the Loch Muir Inn. They were the bait in his trap. He didn't have to wait long. The phone gave a ping and Gallagher's response appeared on its screen.

What?

It wasn't quite the response Hamish had hoped for. It seemed almost as though Gallagher's hearing problem not only made phone calls pointless but also affected how he read messages, too. He decided to make his reply as clear as possible.

Girls here at Loch Muir.

There was a short pause before Gallagher replied.

How?

Hamish typed his response as quickly as he could. Albert, watching over his shoulder, told him to stop.

"I couldn't do one o' these stupid texty things as quick as that," he said. "Slow down or you'll send your reply too fast and he'll smell a rat."

Hamish nodded, picking out the remaining words more slowly before sending the message.

You told me find them. I looked in Lochdubh.
Saw you run out of churchyard. Police and
medics came. Nobody with girls in manse.
I walked in. Got them to come with me.

Gallagher's reply came quickly and was typically concise.

How?

Hamish took his time over the next message.
This, he decided, was like reeling in a fish. He
had it on the line and had to play it carefully if he
wasn't to lose it.

Elena trusts me. I was kind to her. Told her I'd
give back passports and some cash.

Gallagher's next text was his longest yet.

You don't have passports.

Hamish now decided it was time to land his
catch.

I lied. I've closed the place for the day.

He attached the photo of Kira and Elena standing at the bar, their wrists bound. Gallagher sent an immediate reply.

See you at 5.

"Looks like we've got about an hour to wait," Hamish said, "so we may as well relax."

"How about a drink, then?" Blair grunted.

Everyone stared at him as though he'd just belched at the king's coronation.

"A cup o' tea would be grand, Albert," Hamish said, and Albert headed for the kitchen.

Once they were all settled with cups of tea and a generous plate of biscuits, Albert having decided that he might as well empty the tin, Andrew MacDougall spoke again.

"I still don't know why you wanted us all here," he said, leaving his tea untouched.

"There may no' be another chance for us all

to have a wee get-together wi' Mr. Gallagher," Hamish said, enjoying a sip of tea. "I'm pretty sure now that I know everything that's happened, but any of you are welcome to set me right if I get my story a wee bit wrong once Gallagher arrives."

There then came the sound of an outboard motor and Hamish crossed the room to stand near the floor-length curtains, from where he could see out of the window down toward the beach without being seen himself.

"That looks like our man," he said, watching the boat's bow crunch up onto the beach.

"Aye, that's his dinghy all right," said Albert, standing by Hamish's side.

"Okay, everybody out of sight except Albert, Kira and Elena," Hamish ordered. "Albert, you need to greet him as he comes in. Kira and Elena, stay sitting at that table. I'll be in the alcove behind the door. I'll take him down as soon as he's inside."

Jimmy and Blair disappeared into the kitchen with the MacDougalls and the female officer. Looking out the window again, Hamish watched

Gallagher walking up the beach. He was wearing a white T-shirt and loose black jeans with a wide belt that had a fancy buckle. Hamish quickly took his place in the shadows of the alcove and looked out across the room, realizing to his horror that two things were wrong.

Gallagher strutted into the bar, grunted a greeting of sorts to Albert and stared at Kira and Elena, who were no longer wearing cable ties around their wrists. There were also numerous cups and saucers on the tables.

"What's this?" he snarled at Albert. "Some kind o' tea party?"

Hamish moved quickly, slamming into Gallagher from behind and knocking him to the ground, slapping handcuffs on him. Hamish stood up and Gallagher flipped to his feet like a gymnast, aiming a kick which Hamish dodged before grabbing the smaller man by the throat. He looked straight into Gallagher's face, noting the dark bruising in the corner of the smaller man's left eye and the swelling to the eyebrow.

"That'll be where Davey thumped you," he

said through gritted teeth. "Behave yourself or I'll give you a lot worse than that."

Hamish hauled Gallagher across the room and dumped him in a chair just as the others filed back in. Gallagher laughed when he saw the MacDougalls and Jimmy put himself between them and Gallagher, warning them to "Keep the heid." They all took their seats again, facing Gallagher.

"If I'd known it was going to be a family reunion," he said, sneering, "I'd have brought my shotgun."

"Aye, the shotgun's no' licensed, is it, Mick?" Hamish said, pacing the floor between Gallagher and the door. "But that's only one o' the things we're going to be charging you with." We've got you on everything from people trafficking and dangerous driving to the attempted murder o' my constable. The shotgun, however, was involved in an actual murder and that's what I really want to talk about now. You see, Mick, you're a suspect for the murder o' Kathleen Tait, but you're no' the only one. Looking round the room here, I can see six others.

"Let's start wi' your old pal, Hector Mac-Crimmon. You and Hector go way back and, at first, I thought it was too much o' a coincidence for Hector to show up in Lochdubh around the same time that you started making a nuisance o' yourself. Hector, you see, got to meet all sorts o' celebrities when he was a boxer—"

"A boxer?" Gallagher laughed. "That auld fart couldn't punch the scum off the top o' one o' those piss-poor pints he serves."

Hector squirmed slightly in his chair, glowering at Gallagher, but saying nothing.

"As well as celebrities, Hector mixed wi' some shady characters down south in Glasgow. We know there are gangsters down there who would dearly love to have caught up wi' you and Kathleen. Was Hector their hitman? It was a theory, but no' one that held any water. Hector had a cast-iron alibi—he was playing his pipes at the head o' a parade when Kathleen was murdered. Also, the pathologist said the murderer didn't have big hands, and Hector has hands like snow shovels. Hector is just what he says he is—a man looking for a quiet life running a village pub. He was

genuinely horrified to see you in his new neigh-
borhood, but you were happy to see him. You
decided you could use him. You set him up wi' a
story about the MacDougalls wanting you dead.
I'm thinking that was all to do wi' you having
decided to disappear. The MacDougalls were
looking for you, right enough, and I reckon you
were lucky they never got to you afore now.

"So who are my other suspects? What about
your wife? Shona certainly had a motive for kill-
ing Kathleen. As far as Shona was concerned,
Kathleen had stolen her husband. Kathleen had
poisoned your mind against her, turning you
into a maniac who would turn violent and punch
her in the face. Made a terrible mess wi' those
nasty rings o' yours. Shona also has small hands,
which would fit the strangulation marks, but
would she have had the opportunity to commit
murder? I doubt it. After what you did to her,
Mick, Shona doesn't like to leave the house. Her
father told us she was at home on the afternoon
of the murder, and the neighbors around where
they live are, what you might call, 'vigilant.' I'm
sure they can confirm she was home all day.

"What about Shona's father? Andrew left me in no doubt what he would do to you if he ever caught up with you, Mick..."

"In his dreams!" Gallagher let out a derisive snort. Andrew MacDougall made to stand up but Shona hauled him back into his seat.

"But Andrew's problem was with you, Mick, not Kathleen. Why would he want to kill her? Maybe he was trying to force her to tell him where you were. That's possible. Andrew doesn't have big hands like Hector, but he's strong from years of working wi' stone, so it would be easy for him to get carried away wi' the strangling and...take it too far. So does he have an alibi? Well, he says he was out walking in the hills at the time o' the murder, and that could be true, but he knew exactly where Kathleen lived. You see, Andrew worked on the drystane dyke around a house close to Kathleen's. He likely saw Gallagher at her house. He would know how to cross the hills and arrive at the house unseen. Andrew, then, remains a suspect.

"That brings us to James MacDougall. Like his father, James had made threats against you, Mick..."

Gallagher sniggered and, if looks were like bolts of lightning, James would have left Gallagher roasted to a crisp. Yet James could also see Hamish wagging a warning finger at him and he remained in his seat.

"...and like his father," Hamish continued, "James knew where Kathleen lived and how to reach the house without being spotted. Neither does he have an alibi. We could find no hotel where his father told us he was working on a boiler. So where was James on the afternoon of the murder? Well, we know for sure that he had been scouring the coast looking for the *Millennium Falcon*, Mick. My constable traced two anonymous calls about your boat to James's phone. I think James was out there on coast watch looking for you, Mick. I don't think he cared about Kathleen and James is a bit bigger than his dad. I think the size of his hands probably rules him out as a suspect."

"He doesn't have the guts to kill anyone," Gallagher said, baring his teeth at James.

"Take care there, Mick," Hamish warned. "If all this lot come piling over here to have a go at you, I won't be able to stop them. Don't forget you're in cuffs as well."

"Cuffs or no'," Gallagher stated boldly, "I'm no' feared o' any o' them!"

"Maybe best mind your manners anyway," Hamish told him. "That brings us to Kira and Elena. We know they were at the murder scene. We have their fingerprints in the house and in the victim's car, as well as Kira's prints on the shotgun. So how did they come to be there? From what they've told us, Kira and Elena were running away from you, Mick. Little did they know that Kathleen was your partner in crime. She was cruising the road looking for the girls, picked them up without them suspecting a thing, and took them back to her place. Kira and Elena have been reluctant to say much more, but I think I've worked it out. I think Kathleen was holding them at gunpoint when you phoned, Mick. We checked her phone. She had a call from you that went unanswered.

"Kira used the distraction o' the phone ringing to grab the shotgun and they wrestled for it. We have an eyewitness saw Elena run out and start the car. Then the gun went off and blew an armchair to bits. Kira, you used that shock to do this..."

Hamish held both hands at chest height, as though clasping the shotgun across his body. He jerked his right hand upward.

"You whacked Kathleen in the face wi' the butt o' the shotgun. You broke her jaw—doubtless knocked her senseless, but did you then have time to put your hands around her neck and strangle her before you ran out to join Elena in the car?"

"No, no!" Kira said, bursting into tears. "I not strangle..."

"The evidence against Kira is pretty strong, is it no', Mick?" Hamish said, turning to Gallagher, "but we still have you to consider. Can we add murder to your long list o' crimes?

"Kathleen Tait was your partner. The two o' you were a couple, even though you weren't supposed to be seeing each other anymore. She was also your business partner. We heard a woman worked on the *Millennium Falcon* wi' you—most likely Kathleen. On the afternoon o' her murder, when she told you she had Kira and Elena at her place, you raced up there. You saw her car and Elena driving, so you forced it off the road, but the girls got away. Then, rather than hang around wi' a witness watching, you drove straight to Kathleen's house.

"When you got there, the place was a shambles and you could see Kathleen was in a bad way. Was she dead? I think not. I'm guessing she was barely conscious. You found your wallet and the girls' passports. You probably thought that, wi' the gun having gone off, somebody nearby might have called the police, so you had to get out of there—but what about Kathleen? She needed help. Did you help her, Mick?

"No—you put your hands round her throat. You have small hands, don't you? I doubt she would have been able to put up much of a fight. You squeezed the life out o' a defenseless woman and left her there on the floor o' her house. Aye, that's the story I'm going for, Mick. You see, the pathologist not only told us the murderer had small hands, but there were other marks on Kathleen's neck. Those marks were caused by your rings, weren't they, Mick? The marks will match yon rings perfectly. Why did you kill her, Mick? Why did you no' just take her wi' you in your car? Was she able to speak when she saw you in the room? What did she say, Mick? What could that poor woman possibly have said to make you kill her?"

"What did she say?" Mick yelled, his eyes full of hate. "What did she no' say? She was ay saying something to wind me up! Even wi' a broken jaw she still had a go at me—telling me how crazy I was to bring those lassies into the country. She told me she'd had enough and that we had to pack it in. She kept calling me an eejit and telling me it was all over. Well, it was for her! I got her by the throat and shut her up for good! I killed the stupid cow and I'm glad I'll never have to hear her moaning at me ever again!"

"Thank you, Mick," Hamish said, standing close to Gallagher. "Now we're taking you in for murder."

"Aye, right!" Gallagher roared, leaping to his feet and spreading his arms. The handcuffs dangled from one wrist and he dropped a thin sliver

340

of metal on the floor. "You'll no' be taking me anywhere!"

"Clever," Hamish said looking down at the thin steel tool. "You must have had that tucked inside the back o' your belt to undo the cuffs."

"It's no' my first time in handcuffs!" Gallagher laughed. His free hand flew to his belt buckle and produced a short but viciously sharp knife.

"And that must be the blade you used on Davey," Hamish said, tensing himself for Gallagher's next move.

"Get in my way now and you'll be next," Gallagher warned. "I'm walking out o' here!"

There was a metallic click of a telescopic baton being extended and Gallagher glanced behind him to see the female officer standing poised, the baton raised, ready to strike. She pointed at the knife with her open hand.

"Put the knife—" she began, but got no further before Gallagher launched a high kick as quick as a striking snake. He caught her in the chest, sending her flying back over a table. He then turned to Hamish, who also now had his baton ready, stepped forward and swung the blade. Hamish dodged the knife and smashed his baton into Gallagher's wrist. Gallagher howled with pain and tried to slash the open prong of the handcuffs at Hamish's face but Hamish was too quick for him, grabbing Gallagher's injured wrist in an arm lock and punching him full in the face. Then he punched him again, and again, and had drawn his fist back for another when he heard Jimmy's voice.

"Enough, laddie," Jimmy said quietly, grabbing Hamish's wrist. "He's out o' it."

Hamish released the arm lock and Gallagher slumped to the floor, groaning. The female officer picked herself up off the floor, marched across and roughly grabbed Gallagher's injured arm, slapping the handcuff back on. He let out a yelp of pain. Hamish crouched down beside them.

"You okay?" he asked the officer. She nodded. He removed Gallagher's belt. "Just in case he's got any more wee tricks in here."

"What were you on about there?" Blair said, deeming it safe for him to approach. "Yon pathologist's report said nothing about ring marks."

"Did it no'?" Hamish replied. "Maybe I made

that wee bit up. It was worth it for the confession, though. Wi' so many suspects, a confession is the best thing in court."

"You won't see this man in any regular court," Chief Superintendent Farnham appeared, followed by several very large, able-looking men in suits. "He'll end up behind bars, but I'll be taking care of that side of things from now on."

He instructed two of his men to drag Gallagher to his feet.

"He needs to see a medic," Hamish complained.

"I'll take care of that, too," Farnham said, turned and left, followed by his men who half-marched, half-carried Gallagher out the door. Hamish stared after him, running his hand through his hair. Where the hell had Farnham suddenly sprung from?

Jimmy then took charge of the scene in the pub, calling in his own officers who escorted Kira, Elena and Albert out to waiting police vehicles. The MacDougalls left under their own steam, Andrew pausing at the door of the pub to nod a silent farewell to Hamish.

Eventually, just Hamish and Blair were left

343

in the bar. Blair poured them each a whisky and they clinked glasses.

"It was you, I suppose," Hamish said, "who told Farnham we were here?"

"Observe and report back to him," Blair said. "That was my job here."

"And Farnham will get Gallagher locked up?"

"You can bet on it. He'll make sure that Gallagher never walks free again. That means I'm done here. Now I can head home and hope never to set foot in this part o' the world again."

"I can't say I'll miss you," Hamish said, "but it would be interesting to see whether Jekyll or Hyde comes out on top."

"What in the name o' the wee man are you talking about?"

"Never mind," Hamish said. "Away you go now. I've to wait here until my pal Dougie brings a trailer to take Gallagher's dinghy away."

Hamish waited by the dinghy until he was sure everyone else had gone, then clambered aboard and started the engine. He headed along the shore of the loch and, after a few minutes, spotted what he was looking for—the old boathouse.

He tied the dinghy alongside the remains of an ancient jetty that was now little more than a set of rotting wooden steps, and climbed up to what looked like a small stone barn. The wooden door was secured with a padlock and chain, which did not survive the impact of Hamish's boot.

Inside the boathouse, it was dark and musty. He pulled out his flashlight and picked out a camp bed and sleeping bag along with a small stove. This was where Gallagher had been hiding out. Then his flashlight beam picked up a stack of six cardboard boxes. Hamish examined the contents and was delighted to find that each contained half a dozen bottles of high-end whisky.

"Michty me!" he muttered to himself, patting the first box. "You'll do handsomely for that drink I owe Alistair and his coastguard crew. I'll have to make some cupboard space in my kitchen for the rest!"

A few nights later, once things had quieted down almost back to normal in Lochdubh, Hamish sat with Claire at their favorite table in the Napoli.

They were sharing a bottle of wine and thinking about ordering food, although Willie had told them to take all the time they wanted to "bruise the menu." Hamish wasn't sure whether he meant "browse" or "peruse" but decided it didn't really matter.

"This is nice," Claire said. "I like it when it's just us."

"Aye, me too," Hamish agreed, "and we can enjoy it for a while longer. Davey will no' be back to work for a couple o' months, Elspeth has gone back to Glasgow and even Priscilla has flown south for the winter, back to London."

"What will happen to Kira and Elena?"

"They'll be handed ower to the immigration people," Hamish said. "They have passports, but they entered the country illegally. Then there was the minor stuff—stealing and suchlike. I'm guessing they'll be deported back to Latvia."

"And what about us?" Claire asked. "Are we going to be leaving the country any time soon? You did say you would think about it."

"Aye, and I have been," Hamish replied. "I've sorted something out for when Davey gets back."

"Really?" Claire was surprised and starting to feel excited. "Where are we going? Tenerife? That's good for some winter sun."

"Well, no' quite," Hamish said. "You know I've a friend in Chicago?"

"Aye," Claire replied, looking slightly crestfallen. "He's been here a couple o' times. James Bland, isn't it?"

"That's him," Hamish said. "He told me we could use his place."

"Hamish," Claire said with tinge of disappointment. "I'm sure his house in Chicago is very nice but we talked about getting some sunshine to warm us through the winter and the winter in Chicago is even colder than it is here."

"Och, we're no' going to stay at his house there," Hamish explained. "James says we can use his villa just outside Nassau in the Bahamas. It's got its own swimming pool and—"

"The Bahamas!" Claire shrieked. "But that's... that's fantastic! I've never been anywhere like... I mean... It's magic! I can't wait!"

"Well, obviously you have to wait until Davey's back," Hamish said, teasing her, "but I can book our flights tomorrow morning if you want."

"If I want?" Claire laughed. "Of course I want! Hamish Macbeth, you're a...you're a..."

"I think the words you're looking for are 'an absolute gem,'" he said, grinning.

"Aye, you're that all right," she said and leaned over the table to kiss him. "An absolute gem."

About the Authors

M. C. Beaton, hailed as the "Queen of Crime" by the *Globe and Mail,* was the author of the *New York Times* and *USA Today* bestselling Agatha Raisin novels—the basis for the hit series on Acorn TV and public television—as well as the Hamish Macbeth series. Born in Scotland, Beaton started her career writing historical romances under several pseudonyms as well as her maiden name, Marion Chesney. Her books have sold more than 22 million copies worldwide.

A long-time friend of M. C. Beaton's, **R. W. Green** has written numerous works of fiction and nonfiction. He lives in Surrey with his family and a black Labrador called Ossian.